THE NIGHTINGALE MOON

by Nicholas Sweedo

LITTLE CREEK PRESS®
A DIVISION OF KRISTIN MITCHELL DESIGN, LLC

Mineral Point, Wisconsin USA

Published by Little Creek Press®
A Division of Kristin Mitchell Design, LLC
5341 Sunny Ridge Road
Mineral Point, Wisconsin 53565

Cover Illustration: Michael Kress-Russick
Editor: Carl Stratman
Book Design: Little Creek Press

Limited First Edition
April 2014

Cover Illustration copyright © 2014 Michael Kress-Russick

Printed in Wisconsin, United States of America.

For more information or to order books:
www.littlecreekpress.com

Library of Congress Control Number: 2014934957

ISBN-10: 0989978028
ISBN-13: 978-0-9899780-2-6

To Caroline

PROLOGUE

The king walked down the long hallway through the castle on his way to the meeting room. It was of great risk for him to be here, and through his head ran thoughts of the danger he might face. Suddenly, he heard a noise and reached for his sword, only to be embarrassed when he came face to face with the perpetrator: a giant blackbird that perched on the nearby window.

He continued in solitude until he reached the end of the hallway. *Last chance to turn back.* He took a deep breath and struck his fist firmly against the wooden door.

It was opened by another king, the one to whom the castle belonged. The host king warmly greeted the visitor and thanked him for accepting his invitation and for agreeing to come alone, for what the host king had to say was revolutionary.

The visiting king hesitantly returned the host's greeting and walked through the door. He was stunned to see in front of him, sitting at the round table, the presence of two more kings. His three greatest rivals, all in one place. Now he knew he had made a mistake, for this had to be a trap. Nevertheless, he walked into the center of the room to hear what the three kings had to say. ♣

For one night, all was right with the world. The setting sun had just about lost its battle with the man in the moon, and the jutting red rocks seemed to touch the stars. Off in the distance, a coyote added its voice to the symphony of owls, crickets, and rattlesnakes. Nightingale leaned over and gave his horse Raindrop a pat. In all his travels he hardly remembered such a beautiful evening. The painted desert, now washed by the moonlight and the stars, had a silver tint that was breathtaking. Soon it would be time to make camp, for cold air comes quickly to a desert night.

Nightingale rode past some cactuses and came to a ledge in a rocky hillside overlooking a distant town. Tomorrow he would ride into the town to eat and win more money. But tonight it was time to rest. Adjacent to the ledge was a small cave that would provide the perfect shelter. Though sleeping under the stars was a nice thought, it was getting cold and there were many creatures about.

He dismounted Raindrop and was about to walk down to the shelter when he heard a noise. He turned around and saw a mountain lion that was no more than one leap away. He had never been this close to one before. She was sleek and nimble-looking; if he were not scared for his life, he would have reflected in admiration of her.

Fortunately, when the pressure was on, Nightingale was at his best. He had a talent for keeping his emotions under control and projecting confidence even when he had none. It was one of the main reasons, along with his instincts and natural intelligence, that he was a great cardplayer, for he could keep his cool and maintain his poker face even when his adrenaline was rising.

He took a deep breath and then shifted his weight forward while staring directly into the eyes of the wild creature. She took a step toward him, but he held his ground and then took a step forward himself. He felt chills running down his spine, but he fought the urge to cringe and instead stood even taller. Now he felt empowered and confident. The lion felt this shift in energy, and she turned and walked away. On this night, the bird spirit within him was truly a match for the lion.

Nightingale worked his way down to the cave which was big enough for him and Raindrop. He built a fire and then lay down with the lights of the town a distant backdrop. He closed his eyes and listened. Sometimes he thought he could hear her voice calling him in the night. He could still remember her face, and that made him happy.

He opened his eyes, reached into his pocket, and pulled out the card. It was his most important possession, valuable to no one but himself. He looked at the card, the Jack of Diamonds, and touched its face. His mother had given it to him and told him it was very special, and he treated it with honor. For him it was good luck, and he felt that by carrying it around, he kept her spirit always with him. Rest up, he told himself. There was a big day ahead.

♙

He awoke with a start. He heard Raindrop neighing in distress from outside the cave. He leapt to his feet and scampered out of the cave and up the hill. "Uh-oh," he said when he reached the top. The mountain lion was back, and she had brought a friend. ♣

The two lions slowly encircled the horse and looked ready to pounce. Nightingale acted quickly, for there was no time to think. He sprinted past the lions and jumped on Raindrop's back. He gave her a swift kick, and the steed quickly galloped right through the lions' circle and back down the hill.

When he got to the cave, Nightingale realized this was not the best plan, for if the lions followed he would be trapped with nowhere to go. It did not take long for his fear to become reality as the lions briskly descended down the hill. He looked up at the lions about to pounce and wondered if this was the end.

Suddenly a rock came out of nowhere and hit one of the lions right between the eyes. Before Nightingale could process what was happening, a second rock hit the other mountain lion with such force that both cats decided they had had enough. They turned away from the ledge and made their way down the hillside.

Nightingale ran out of the cave and turned to see a boy a little older than he smiling and holding a slingshot. "Lucky for you I'm the best shot in the West!" the boy said happily. Nightingale climbed up the hill and got a better look at his rescuer under the moonlight. He looked about fourteen or fifteen and had dark, wavy hair and brown eyes. He extended his hand and said, "Hi, I'm Jack."

"I'm Nightingale, but you can call me Gale."

Jack shook his hand and sized up the boy in front of him. He seemed to be a little younger, maybe twelve, and looked like an Indian, but he had the bluest eyes Jack had ever seen.

"Pleasure to meet you, Gale," Jack said.

"Would you like to warm up by my fire?" Gale asked.

"Absolutely," Jack responded. "It's cold out here."

They walked with their horses down the hill into the cave where the fire was crackling. Gale took out a knife and got to work on carving a bow. He had started on it a month ago and was now putting on the finishing touches.

Jack, meanwhile, was sitting up on the ledge and quietly admiring the breathtaking view. A few minutes later he reached into his pack and pulled out a pack of jerky and offered some to Gale.

Gale put down the bow and joined Jack out on the ledge. "You saved my life," Gale said in between bites of jerky. "What were you doing out here?"

"I made camp about a half mile from here. I saw those mountain lions heading over toward the cliff and then I heard your horse, so I figured I'd go see what was happening."

"Your aim was incredible. Where'd you learn to shoot like that?"

"I've always had great aim, whether I'm using a slingshot, a bow, a pistol, or just my arm. When I'm bored, I just use whatever's around to practice."

"Well, I'm glad you stopped by. Are you from around here?" Gale asked.

"No, I'm from back East. I came to New Mexico territory to look for my brother."

Jack looked out into the valley, marveling at the magnificent desert scene complete with red rocks, the moon, and stars. "You sure don't see anything like this in Pennsylvania," he said.

"That's one place I haven't been," Gale said as he knelt over the fire. "So why are you looking for your brother out here?"

"He joined the Union army and was stationed in the desert, but then his unit got into a skirmish with the Rebels and he was captured. Somehow he managed to sneak a letter out to us, and it said he was being held prisoner at Fort McCaffrey, a remote Confederate base near here. My parents were distraught, and I told them I would go rescue him. They said no—I was too young and they didn't want anything to happen to me too. Well, I wasn't going to just sit around and do nothing. I was too young to join the army, and if I couldn't fight to save the Union and free the slaves, the least I could do was save my older brother."

"So you ran away from home?"

"Yes, I left in the middle of the night and made my way to Philadelphia, where I caught a train to Kansas City and then Santa Fe. I bought a horse and went to find my brother, Marco."

"Did you find him?"

"No. The fort was deserted. The only person I saw was an old Mexican man sitting outside, and when I asked if he knew where the prisoners were, he started rambling about Confederate ghosts and evil queens. He seemed to be a few cards short of a full deck. In any case, I don't know where my brother is. I have no idea. He could be anywhere, so there's nothing more I can do. Anyway, the war's almost over. For all I know he's free and home by now."

Jack turned to look at Gale. "So what's your story? What are you doing out here all by yourself?" Jack asked.

"I'm a poker player. I go from town to town and play. I survive off my winnings."

Jack had a look of surprise. "Really? How long have you been doing that?"

"Since I was seven."

"That's amazing! Who do you get to play with you?"

"Usually it's some townspeople that take pity on me. Poor orphaned Indian boy. I don't always win but I'm pretty good."

"Orphan, huh?" Jack said. "Sorry to hear that."

"My mother taught me to play cards," Gale said. "Do you play?"

"Oh yeah, big time. I've played some poker, écarté, and faro, but my game of choice is *Hearts*."

"Hearts? I haven't heard of that."

"Really? That's the game my family always plays. I'm the best player in my town. In fact, I've never played anyone better than I am. Tomorrow I will teach you the rules."

"Sure, I'm always up for a new game. How about tomorrow we ride into town and see what we can find?"

"It's a deal," Jack said. "I've got time for a game before I head home."

And with that, the two boys wished each other good night and then drifted off to sleep. A moment later, a shooting star sped across the sky over the howling coyote on the red rocks and toward the man in the moon far, far away. ♣

he next morning, the boys rode their horses down the main street of the small Western town.

"So how do you normally find a game?" Jack asked as they rode past a bank and a general store.

"I normally start at the saloon. It helps that I'm twelve. They think I'm an easy mark."

"Have you seen any gunfights? We hear about all that stuff back East."

"I haven't, though there was a fistfight between two of the players at my table last month. But the marshal was there and he put a stop to it pretty quick."

They pulled up to the Dry Gulch Saloon, tethered their horses outside and strolled through the batwing doors. The melodies of a piano, rich in harmonics, wafted out into the dusty street. There were a few people sitting at the bar and the surrounding tables, and a card game was going on quietly in the corner. Meanwhile, a few ladies were taking it all in from the second floor balcony.

As Jack and Gale surveyed the scene, the music and idle chatter came to a screeching halt. "Do they normally react like this?" Jack wondered aloud.

"Yep," Gale said.

Conspicuous at a table off to the side was a distinguished gentleman with a wide-brimmed hat, finely tailored suit, thick and lengthy mustache, and—most notably—two shiny, silver revolvers pinned to his waist. He was sitting with a few old-timers, and they seemed to be enjoying the day. He turned to one of the old-timers and said wryly, "It's like the old joke, an Indian and an Italian walk into a bar." He then looked directly at Gale and Jack. "What can I do for you boys?"

"We're looking for a game of poker," Gale said. "Is this a place where we can find one?"

"That depends," the man said.

"Yes?" Gale said.

"On whether it's all right with your mother."

The other men at the table let out a good laugh.

Gale stood confidently. "It's only all right with my mother if I win, which I always do."

"Well, it appears the gauntlet has been thrown," the man said. "Pull up a chair." He extended his hand and said, "The name's Hickok. William Hickok."

"Wild Bill Hickok!" Jack said in amazement. "I've read about you in magazines! I can't believe—"

He stopped himself in mid-sentence, for there was a change in the others in the room, a sudden presence of fear, as Hickok's face hardened with menace. Jack paused for a moment and then realized what he had done. "I'm sorry, sir, I didn't mean any disrespect."

"It's OK, son," Hickok said with a smile. "I was just messing with you. I actually like the nickname, but don't tell anybody else that."

Jack was a little starstruck by being in the presence of the legendary lawman, but he gathered himself together and shook Hickok's hand. "I'm Gianni Porelli, but you can call me Jack. This is my friend Gale."

Hickok shook Gale's hand and then turned to Jack. "So what's your game, soldier?"

"I'm not much of a poker player, sir. I guess five-card draw would be my preference, but really I'm more of a Hearts player."

"Ah, Hearts, the game of kings," Hickok said. "It just so happens I'm a Hearts legend. I've only lost once in my life." It was hard to tell if he was serious or just making fun of Jack's game of choice.

Hickok continued. "If I wasn't responsible for maintaining justice in this godforsaken town, I'd be off to St. Louis next week for the Big River Hearts Tournament."

"We could play now, but we'd have to teach him the rules," Jack said pointing at Gale. "He's never played before."

"Well, let's do it then," Hickok said. "Thomas, you stay here and play with us. Fletcher, Saunders, why don't you vacate the table and make room for the real men." Two of the old-timers got up and found some nearby chairs, while Thomas remained at the table. Gale and Jack sat down so that Jack was on Gale's immediate right, Hickok was on Gale's left, and Thomas was directly across.

"So, Mr. Jack," Hickok said, "go on and tell your friend the rules."

Jack turned to Gale. "Just like poker, it's every man for himself. All the cards are dealt evenly with each player getting thirteen. Before play begins, each person passes three cards of his choice to another player. Pass left on the first hand, pass right on the second, pass across on the third, and no pass on the fourth. On the fifth hand, pass left again and repeat the pattern. Only one catch: you can't look at the cards that you're receiving until you've passed your three.

"After the pass, the game begins with whoever has the 2 of Clubs, and then play proceeds in a clockwise direction. After each person plays a card, that's called a trick, and the person who played the highest card of the suit that was first led wins the trick and obtains all four cards that were played. Then they get to lead the next trick with whatever card they want.

"So getting back to the first trick where the 2 of Clubs is led—if you're up next and you have a club, you have to follow suit. If you don't have a club, you can play any card you want. Except you can't play hearts or the Black Maria on the first trick. You also can't lead hearts until a heart has been played on the lead of another suit or until the Maria has been thrown. Are you with me so far?"

"Yeah," Gale said. "Everything except the Black Maria. What's that?"

Suddenly things got quiet, and Hickok said, "That's the vile Jezebel, the evilest woman that ever walked the earth. She'd kill your mother and marry your father. I'm talking, of course, about the Queen of Spades."

"Oh," Gale said, not knowing what to make of the dramatic description.

Jack resumed his explanation. "Let's talk about scoring. At the end of a hand, all the cards have been played for a total of thirteen tricks in all. Whoever captures the Black Maria gets 13 points, and points are bad. Each heart captured is worth 1 point. And Johnny Diamonds is worth 10 negative points—a good card."

Even Hickok seemed surprised by this. "Johnny Diamonds?" he inquired.

"It's what we in my family call the Jack of Diamonds. It's the most valuable card in the deck. Not quite an equal antidote to the evil Queen, but close. And of course, there's always a trip to the moon."

"A trip to the moon?" Gale asked. No wonder he never heard of this game. It was bizarre.

"Shooting the moon," Jack said. "Every player's dream hand, and a nightmare for the others. When you take in every heart, the Black Maria, and Johnny Diamonds, you've shot the moon. Very hard to do. As a result, you get minus 10 points for Johnny and then the choice of adding 26 points to everyone's score or subtracting another 26 from yours. Either way, it's a 36 point swing between you and the field."

"I think I got it," Gale said. "Not sure I have a good feel for the strategy, but I'll give it a shot."

"Just don't give me the Queen, kid," Hickok said with a smile, pointing to the gun on his right hip.

"I forgot to mention," Jack added, "that if you don't take any tricks the entire hand, you get minus 5 points unless someone else shoots the moon. The game can be played to any score. We usually go to 75. When one player reaches that score, the player with the least amount of points wins. How does that sound?"

"Excellent," said Hickok. "Now let's play some cards." He picked up the nearby deck and started to deal. ♣

ale noticed that no one else picked up their cards until they were all dealt, so he observed the etiquette of the table. When he finally did look at his cards, he saw a good low hand. He would not be taking in a lot of tricks, but there were two problems: he only had two spades, and one of them was the Queen.

He did not have the kind of instincts that came with experience in this game, but he was enough of a cardplayer that he could smell danger when it was nearby. The lack of spades was a problem because if other players led spades early on, he would be forced to throw his Queen.

Gale selected three cards to pass, including the Queen of Spades, and slid them over to Hickok on his left. He looked at Jack who was still thinking. Finally, Jack took three cards and confidently passed them over to Gale. Jack had a slight smile on his face, which Gale interpreted to mean that he was in trouble.

Sure enough, when he picked up the cards, he was greeted by the

King of Clubs, the Queen of Hearts, and worst of all, the Ace of Spades. He glared at Jack, who returned an expression that seemed to say, "Sorry to do that to you on your very first hand."

Thomas won the first trick and then started leading spades. On the third trick, Gale was forced to throw his Ace since it was his only spade left. He grimaced slightly as he threw the card, for he knew what was coming. Hickok threw down the Queen that Gale had passed, and Gale won sole possession of the Black Maria with his Ace high.

That was the last trick Gale took in the round. Hickok ended up with the Jack of Diamonds and three hearts for a score of minus 7. Thomas took ten hearts for a score of 10, Jack took no tricks for a score of minus 5, and Gale was sitting in last place with a straight 13 from the Queen of Spades. "Not so bad for your first hand, Gale," Jack said.

"No thanks to you," Gale remarked.

⚑

The game went on and things did not get any better for Gale, for he just could not stop getting the Queen. He was able to land Johnny a few times along with the Jezebel, but his point total was going up, not down. Thomas was behind him in score; he had not had any really bad takes but no good ones either. Jack and Hickok were battling it out for the top spot—Jack with several no-trick hands, and Hickok with some timely Johnny grabs.

Hickok tried to shoot the moon on one hand, and the game would have been over if not for a clever stop by Jack. After the near moon, the score stood with Hickok at 9, Jack at 24, Thomas at 45, and Gale at 72, only three points away from ending the game.

Hickok glanced at Thomas's scoresheet and then turned to the boys.

"Let's raise the stakes, shall we?" he said.

"Shouldn't be hard," Gale said, "since there aren't any stakes at the moment."

"Win this match," Hickok continued while looking at Jack, "and I'll stake you at the Big River Tournament next week. You're playing well, and I'd love to see you win that tournament since I can't be there this year to win it myself."

Jack returned his gaze. "It's a deal, but only if you pay for Gale to play too."

"Fair enough," Hickok said. "But you have to beat me, and remember, I've only lost once before."

It was Hickok's turn to deal, and the pass was to the left. Once all the cards were dealt, Gale looked at his hand. It was a good low hand that included the Jack of Diamonds. There were only two spades, however, which could be trouble if he was passed the Ace, King, or Queen of Spades. But Jack was on his right, and Jack wouldn't pass him a high spade at this stage of the game, would he?

The passes were complete, and Gale picked up the cards Jack had passed him. They were the King, Queen, and Jack of Spades! *What?* Gale wondered. It made no sense to him. Jack should not have passed him the King or the Queen since he was so close to busting out. And why would he pass the Jack of Spades? It was a useful card to help smoke out the Queen.

Suddenly, it hit him. He looked over at Jack and they exchanged conspiratorial glances. It was brilliant, really, Gale thought. Jack probably did not have many spades and would have stood a good chance of eating the Queen had he kept them. He figured Gale would likely have a few spades, so he passed the Queen along with *both* of his other spades to give Gale a little extra protection.

Now that Gale had five spades, he could exhibit a bit of control over where the Queen went. Not only was Hickok in the lead, but he had now promised to fund their entry fee to the Big River Hearts Tournament, so there was more reason than ever to go after him.

After the pass, the hands were:

Gale:
Clubs: None
Diamonds: J, 10, 8, 5, 4, 2
Spades: K, Q, J, 8, 4
Hearts: J, 4

Hickok:
Clubs: A, Q, 8, 7, 6, 2
Diamonds: K
Spades: A, 9, 6, 5, 3, 2
Hearts: None

Thomas:
Clubs: J
Diamonds: A, 9, 3
Spades: 10, 7
Hearts: K, 9, 8, 7, 5, 3, 2

Jack:
Clubs: K, 10, 9, 5, 4, 3
Diamonds: Q, 7, 6
Spades: None
Hearts: A, Q, 10, 6

Hickok led with the 2 of Clubs, Thomas responded with the Jack of Clubs, Jack played the King, and Gale threw the 8 of Diamonds. The lack of clubs got Hickok's attention, and the lawman looked at Gale with a hint of surprise. Gale had considered throwing the Jack of Diamonds to help Jack, but he did not want to play that card yet, for he might need the card himself if he busted with Hickok still in the lead.

It was now Jack's lead, and he led the 3 of Clubs. Here he was going to see how good Gale was—or how patient, really. For if Gale laid the Queen of Spades, there was no guarantee Hickok would take it. Gale proved Jack's faith in him to be well-placed, for he played the 5 of Diamonds. Hickok followed with the 8 of Clubs, and Thomas surprised everyone by playing the 7 of Hearts.

Two players without clubs! Hickok knew he had to stay away from clubs, so he led the 9 of Spades, hoping to fish out the Queen. Thomas played the 10, Jack played the Ace of Hearts, and Gale took the trick with the King of Spades. Now he was at 73 points—only two away from busting.

Gale led the 4 of Hearts, Hickok threw the Ace of Clubs, Thomas played the 3 of Hearts, and Jack happily took the trick with the Queen of Hearts and hoped that Gale had noticed the same thing that he had seen.

Jack led the 4 of Clubs, and it now was Gale's turn. He knew that the 4 of Clubs was the lowest club left, since the 2 and 3 had already been played. He also knew that Thomas had no clubs. Therefore, if he threw the Queen, Hickok would certainly take it unless Jack had every single remaining club which was unlikely. Gale threw down the Queen of Spades. Hickok scowled and laid the 6 of Clubs. Thomas tossed the 9 of Hearts to add to Hickok's miserable trick.

"The 6 of Clubs," Hickok muttered as he pulled in the cards.

Hickok now played the 7 of Clubs, Thomas threw the 8 of Hearts, Jack played the 10 of Clubs, and Gale threw the Jack of Diamonds to complete the team effort. Jack was now at minus 6 for the hand and Hickok was at plus 15. Jack was in the lead by 6 points. If Gale got two more hearts, the game would be over and Jack would win.

Jack led the 6 of Hearts, Gale played the Jack, Hickok played the Queen of Clubs, and Thomas played the 5 of Hearts. The game was now effectively over, and Jack had won.

They played out the rest of the hand. At the end, Hickok seemed angry. "You were working together. You think I didn't see that?"

Jack and Gale looked at each other, not knowing what to say, when suddenly Hickok's mood lightened.

"I'm just kidding with you," he said. "I'm proud of you boys. The fact is, there's nothing in the rules that says you can't team up, just as long as you don't talk openly at the table. If you're smart and you want to win this tournament, you're going to have to work together." ♣

ale was still thinking about the final hand. He was starting to get the hang of this game, and he liked it too. It was fun having control of the hand and dictating what would happen. And they had beaten Hickok, who had lost only one game before.

"Marshall Hickok," Jack said, "is it true you've lost only one game of Hearts before today?"

Hickok nodded. "Absolutely true. And I've played a lot of Hearts in my day."

"Who beat you?" Gale asked.

Hickok took a sip of his whiskey. "You boys ever heard of the Coronado Kid?"

"Sure," Jack said. "I read about you and him in the magazines. You caught him a few months ago. There was a massive gunfight between his crew and your guys, and now he's in jail."

"That's mostly true, except for the part about him in jail," Hickok said.

"Really? What happened?" Jack asked.

"A few years ago, he burst onto the scene. Came from somewhere in Mexico, maybe Spain before that. Charming guy, upper-class. Had an insatiable appetite for money, fine wine, and women. He lived on a hacienda south of the border, and he and his gang would ride up north robbing banks and causing trouble. He and I never crossed paths in those days, but I had heard he was the fastest gun in the West. Of course, others have said that about me as well.

"Then he disappeared for a while. No one knows where he went, but just a few months ago he resurfaced in New Mexico. He and his posse attacked a Confederate military fort."

Jack felt his arms tingling with goose bumps as he thought of his brother. "Why did they attack the fort?" Jack asked.

"I don't know, he wouldn't tell me. I heard about the attack and rode down with some men. We crossed paths at a ghost town just outside the Rio Grande. We killed most of his men, and I disarmed him."

Hickok continued. "After that we made the long ride back. We stopped overnight and played cards by the campfire. There were four of us and one of him so we uncuffed him, and the three of us played Hearts with him while the fourth sat holding a gun.

"He was the most aggressive player I've ever played. Tried to shoot the moon almost every time, and he was good at it too. Sometimes he blew it and took a hit, but it only takes a few moons to build a lead. When you're playing with a shooter, all the other players need to protect against it, and unfortunately my mates weren't quite up to the task."

"So where is he now?" Gale asked.

"Don't know," Hickok answered. "We cuffed him and went to sleep, and then when I woke up, he was gone and all the other men were dead. I think he left me alive to show me he'd gotten the better of me. And now he's fallen off the edge of the world again. But I'll find him. I'll make it my life's work. In a few months, I'm getting reinforcements here, and then I'm leaving to hunt him down. I don't care if I have to go halfway across the world.

"But enough about me. You boys have a train to catch. I'll get your money from the bank and then get you on the two o'clock train to St. Louis. I look forward to reading about your victory in the paper."

And with that, Hickok got up from the table and led the boys out of the saloon. ♣

The young man lay in darkness, looking out the small window in the corner of his cell. It was a terrible place made only slightly more redeeming by the warm, salty scent of the sea and the sight of the moon shining in the sky overhead.

He was optimistic by nature, but he was losing hope that freedom would ever become a reality. It was only a week ago that he had been taken to this mysterious island. In another context, the setting would have been alluring: warm tropical nights, beautiful beaches, and a crystal-clear ocean. But instead he was trapped inside a fortress on top of a cliff overlooking the coast. From the outside, the structure looked like a grand medieval castle.

He was thinking about his home when he heard footsteps outside the cell. He sat up and saw a young boy approach. The boy took out some bread and handed it to him through the bars. The bread looked fresh and delicious.

"Thank you," the young man said as he eagerly stuffed the first chunk of bread in his mouth. "What's your name?"

"I'm Pierre," the boy replied with an accent. "What's yours?"

"I'm Marco. Nice to meet you." Marco extended his right arm through the bars and they shook hands. "What are you doing here?"

"I heard there was a prisoner here, and I wanted to bring you some food."

"Thank you, that's very kind. Do you know where we are?"

"A small island in the Caribbean."

"This whole thing seems like a dream."

"Why are you here?"

"I've been asking myself the same question," Marco said. "From one prison to another. I was fighting for the Union in the American Southwest. My unit surrendered to the Rebels, and I was held captive at a fort until a few months ago, when the fort was attacked in the middle of the night."

"Really? By who?"

"A crew of bandits. Their leader was a tough-looking gunman. He took me into Mexico, and that's where I met her."

"The Queen," said Pierre.

"Yeah, the Queen. I've never seen anyone like her—so beautiful yet evil-looking at the same time. She looks like she came out of a Grimm fairy tale. All that's missing is the poison apple."

Pierre chuckled. "I know what you mean."

Marco continued. "So then we got on a boat and sailed to this island, and I've been in this cell ever since. She wants something that belongs to my family. I don't have it, but I know where it is.

I have no idea why she wants it or how she knows we have it, but I won't tell her anything. She says she'll keep me locked up here until the end of time unless I tell her where it is. The less you know, Pierre, the better. I wouldn't want her to try and force any information out of you."

"Understood."

"So what's your story? What are you doing in this godforsaken place?"

"I had been attending the Canadian missionary school in Port-au-Prince until the Queen's people kidnapped my mother and me and made us her personal slaves. She runs a kingdom here on the island where the slaves harvest the sugarcane day and night, even though slavery was outlawed in the Caribbean long ago.

"My mother escaped last year," Pierre continued. "The Queen took her to the States where she has another compound. Last year my mother was there working in the fields when Moses arrived, Harriet Tubman. Moses grabbed my mother and a few other slaves and led them up north on the Underground Railroad. I'm sure my mother didn't want to leave me, but I'm glad she got away when she had the chance. I know she'll come back for me someday."

"That's quite a story. I'm sorry you couldn't escape but am glad that your mother did."

"Yeah," Pierre said pensively.

"You must know the Queen pretty well," Marco said. "What is she like? She seems crazy to me."

"She is crazy," Pierre said. "And evil. She thinks it's the 1300s. She talks about power and world domination, saying it's part of her family's legacy."

Suddenly the door to the hallway swung open, and there stood the Queen, looking right at them.

Marco immediately felt a chill run through his body as he raised his head to look at the intimidating figure. As usual, she was dressed in full royal regalia, and she wore a golden crown and carried a large scepter.

"Ah, Pierre, are you making a new friend?" she said in a mild German accent as she walked toward them. "You'll have plenty of time to get to know him on our trip to the mainland because it's time for the international Hearts tournament. I've successfully defended my family's honor by winning four straight years—time to make it five!" she exclaimed with a laugh that pierced Marco's ear, causing him to shudder.

She had come in with another man. He was handsome and of average height and build, and he had dark, curly hair and a black mustache. He smiled and nodded his head at Marco but did not say anything.

"Now run along, Pierre, and get started on my dinner," she ordered. Then her terrible gaze swept over to Marco. "And while I'm sailing to victory on the Mississippi, you'll be staying at my American castle. Would you like to hear about my grand plan? I know you'll appreciate it. And you certainly won't live to tell anyone else!" ♣

The boys loaded their horses onto the horse car and then made their way to the passenger car where they found two seats on the left side. They were each $400 richer thanks to Hickok, who had told them the money was courtesy of the Coronado Kid and his reclaimed stash. As the train pulled out of the station, Jack took out a deck of cards and started shuffling out of habit.

"Tell me more about Hearts," Gale said. "What are some of the strategies? What do you look for?"

Jack continued to shuffle. "I was impressed with the way you played. It was really good for your first time. You knew exactly what to do when I passed you those spades."

"I figured you didn't pass them to me so that I could give the Queen back to you."

"That's right," Jack said. "If you can help it, you want to save the Queen for the person with the lowest score. Sometimes you can't help it though, and you have to give it to someone else. At the end of the day, you have to save yourself, especially if you're ready to bust out. Whoever you give the Queen to may not be too happy, but tough luck. You never have to defend your moves to anyone. Sometimes people think they should tell you how to play, but they don't know what you have in your hand."

"What's the best way to get the Jack of Diamonds?" Gale asked.

"Usually you want to have high cards and win it at the end. But high cards also can lead to the Queen of Spades, so you have to be careful. Once the Queen is played, then it's good to save your high cards and try to get the Jack."

"Do you ever try to win no tricks so that you get minus 5 points?"

"Not usually. Unless I have all low cards. Normally, though, it just happens kind of unintentionally."

"And how about shooting the moon? What's the best way to do that?"

"You have to get the right hand," Jack said. "Either a lot of high cards or a lot of one suit. Low hearts make it tough, unless you also have all the high ones. So if you want to stop someone from shooting, pass them a low heart like the 5 or 6. Because once they play that, chances are someone else will win that trick. And like Hickok said, if you think someone's shooting, you should stop it, because it's worth the 3 or 4 points you get to stop someone from getting minus 36."

"There's a lot of strategy," said Gale. "I like it. So you played this a lot in your family?"

"All the time," Jack said. "I'd play with my parents, Marco, friends, neighbors, anyone. It was great fun."

"That's strange what Hickok said about the Coronado Kid attacking the fort. What do you think happened?"

"I don't know," Jack said. "When I got there it was deserted. After this tournament, I'm going home to Pennsylvania. Maybe with luck my brother will already be home."

As Jack remembered his brother, he looked pensively out the window and noticed buffalo grazing on the prairie. Meanwhile, the train rolled on, and Gale drifted off to sleep. ♣

s Gale slept, Jack continued to look out the window. The sun was setting, and lightning bolts had begun rapidly illuminating the golden prairie. It started to rain, and the sound of the falling water against the windowpane was relaxing. Jack closed his eyes and allowed memories of home to enter his mind.

⚔

"Johnny, come home!" Jack yelled as he threw down the Jack of Diamonds in triumph. "Black Jack wins again!" William, one of the other boys in the hay loft, threw down his card in disgust, while Robert and James shook their heads. "Geez Jack, how do you do it?"

"Because I'm the greatest Hearts player in the land! Card player by day, fearsome pirate by night. I'm Black Jack—defender of the free, protector of the weak!"

"Why aren't you Red Jack? After all, you're always talking about how much you love Johnny Diamonds."

Jack pulled out a card from his pocket and showed the others his lucky Jack of Clubs. "Black Jack uses Johnny to get him what he needs, but he's a loyal Club through and through."

"You're crazy!" one of them said, and they all had a good laugh.

Suddenly they heard the loud clanging of church bells. The bells rang on the hour and during service, but now they were ringing without stopping, which usually signified an announcement important enough for the whole town to hear.

Ignoring the ladder, the boys jumped off the loft into the hay and ran out of the barn. There was already a crowd gathered outside the church. The Neffs Church was an impressive building with orange brick, magnificent stained glass windows, and the tallest steeple in Eastern Pennsylvania. It was located at the intersection of three roads that came together to form a Y. Surrounding the church was an old cemetery with gravestones dating back to the eighteenth century.

It was a beautiful spring day. The sun was shining and there was a gentle breeze from the north. The boys ran to the side of the church where there was a small, elevated platform. People were milling about and waiting for the mayor to appear and make an announcement. Jack knew everyone in the small town, and he saw his parents and younger sister toward the back of the gathered crowd.

"What do you think is going on?" James asked. "Is it war?"

"Yeah," Jack said.

Finally Mayor Schumann arrived and got up on the platform. "Good morning, everyone. Yesterday, Fort Sumter in South Carolina fell to the Confederates. I'm here to tell you that we're at war." The crowd was silent, but they were not stunned, for war fever had been building across the nation.

"You all know we have several sons that are training to fight at this very moment," the mayor continued, "and we all must do whatever it takes to support them and the Union. The Union must not fail. If the Declaration of Independence fails here in America, then it fails in the rest of the world, for this time and for all time. We can't let that happen. Everyone has a role they can play, so it's time to get to work. I'll keep you updated with any news that I hear. May God bless us all."

The mayor stepped down off the platform and the crowd began to disperse.

Jack looked back at his parents. His mother had pulled out a handkerchief and was wiping her eyes. "Where's your brother at, Jack?" Robert said.

"Last I heard he was in Harrisburg training with the Pennsylvania 2nd. He volunteered the first chance he had. I wish I could do the same."

"We could run away and enlist," William said. "We'll show those Rebs. They ain't seen nothing like Black Jack!"

"I wish I could, but I can't do that to my parents," Jack said. "They're worried enough about Marco. And I'm only ten. I'd have to lie about my age, and I don't think I'd fool anyone for long."

"Maybe we could be a ring of spies!" James said. "Or a team of heroes like Athos, Porthos, Aramis, and d'Artagnan. All for one and one for all!"

"I gotta do something, that's for sure," Jack said.

They walked back to the barn which had three hex signs painted on the wall outside. The signs were circles with colorful patterns, and their purpose was to ward off evil spirits. They were common in Pennsylvania Dutch communities such as Neffs. The Pennsylvania Dutch were not actually Dutch at all, but rather Deutsche, or German. The Porellis were one of the few Italian families in Neffs, but they fit right in with their Teutonic neighbors, even if their meals more often consisted of fettuccine and prosciutto rather than fastnachts and sauerbraten.

"Another game, Jack?" Robert asked.

"No, thanks. Not in the mood." Jack said farewell to his friends and walked past the barn and into his house where he saw his mother and sister preparing the evening meal. He missed his brother already, and he did not like to think about the possibility of what could happen in a war. His mother turned to him and gave him a big hug.

"Non perderò anche te," she said. "I'm not losing you."

As Jack came out of his reverie, the sky had turned completely black, and the lightning continued to pound away at the distant prairie. It had been four years since his brother had gone to war. He thought of his mother and how worried she must be about both of them. He hated to have left the way he did, but he had needed to try to find Marco. And soon he would be home. Just one stop in St. Louis for a card tournament, and then he would see his family again.

He glanced over at Gale who was sleeping soundly through the storm. Then he reached into his pocket and took out his Jack of Clubs. It was given to him by his father, who had received it from his father. He was told to protect it because it brought good luck. As a result, the Jack of Clubs was his favorite and the source of his alter ego, Black Jack. He looked at the noble face as he had many times before and then stuck the card back in his pocket. He closed his eyes and slowly drifted off to sleep. ♣

The train pulled into St. Louis on Wednesday morning, and the boys eagerly disembarked after a long ride, for they were looking forward to not only moving around but also to playing some cards. The station was bustling and overflowing with noise as hurried travelers seemed to be moving in a thousand different directions.

They went to the stock car to get their horses and then took a minute to survey the grand station. This environment was totally unfamiliar to Gale. He had never ridden a train or been to a city this big.

"Where do we go from here?" he asked.

"Let's head toward the river. The steamboat leaves tonight," Jack said.

"Great idea. Now where's the river?"

Jack laughed. "Good question."

The boys were still standing in the same place taking it all in when they heard a newspaper boy calling out to the crowd, "Extra! Extra! Read all about it! Lee surrenders to Grant at Appomattox! War over! Lee surrenders! War over!"

"Wow," Jack said. "It's over. Thank God." No one on either side had initially expected the War Between the States to last one year, let alone four long, bloody years.

"North, South, they're all the same to me," Gale said. He pointed straight ahead where there were carriages riding into the station. "How about we head that way?"

They walked with their horses toward the open doors. "You mean you didn't care who won?" Jack asked.

"The troubles of white America aren't a big concern to me," Gale answered.

"What about freeing the slaves?" Jack responded.

"Come and free us from our reservations and then I'll share in the good feelings," Gale said.

They continued walking until they reached the end of the station and found themselves outside. In the distance, about half a mile away, they saw the legendary river—the mighty Mississippi. "There she is, the greatest river in the world. You ever been this far East, Gale?"

"Nope, this is all new to me. Let's go check it out." And with that they jumped on their horses and rode toward the mighty river. ♣

 nce they reached the river, they saw the steamboat right away.

"The *Grande Victoria*," Jack said in admiration.

She was a beautiful vessel and looked brand new as the sunlight reflected the poignant red and golden trim surrounding the bright white exterior. A giant paddle wheel extended from the rear of the boat. Across the top of the bow, the words *Grande Victoria* were displayed in gold.

They walked down to the wharf and passed by stands attended to by several merchants selling everything from Persian scarves to Vermont maple syrup. As they approached the boat, they saw a big crowd of people gathered around someone. Joining the crowd, they saw that it was a magician, a young kid just a little older than they were.

He laid a sword on the ground and picked up a deck of cards. "For my next trick," he bellowed, "I need a volunteer. How about you in the back, young man?" He was pointing straight at Gale. Gale hesitantly stepped forward into the circle created by the surrounding onlookers.

"Here I have a deck of cards," the magician said while holding the deck out for everyone to see. "I'm going to give it to this young man to shuffle. What's your name, good sir?"

"Nightingale."

"Ah, the Nightingale, a proud and defiant European bird. Do you come from Europe, Mr. Nightingale? Your blue eyes doth suggest you do!" The crowd laughed in amusement.

"Sure," Gale responded as he shuffled the deck. "I came with my friend Chris Columbus. It was a terribly long voyage." The crowd laughed again.

"Very good, Sir Nightingale. Now as you can see, the deck has been expertly shuffled by my European friend here. Now Nightingale, I want you to pick a card in your head. Any card at all. Whatever first comes to your mind." The magician paused. "Do you have one?"

"Yes," Gale answered.

"Fantastic. Now I want you to think hard on that card. Concentrate with all your might. Now I'm going to take the deck back and pick a card from the middle. With a tap of my magic wand, I select this one, right here," and the magician pulled out a card. "Now Mr. Nightingale, tell me what card you were thinking of."

"Three of spades," Gale answered. It was a lie, but he wanted to have a little fun.

The magician frowned and his shoulders dropped, and the crowd moaned. Gale took pity on him and changed his tune. "Just kidding. I was really thinking of the Jack of Diamonds."

The magician's eyebrows rose and a smile came across his face. "You mean... this Jack of Diamonds?" He turned over the card in his hand to reveal Johnny himself. The crowd cheered, and the magician soaked in the adoration.

"Guess you got me," Gale said to the magician before walking back toward Jack and the horses.

"Nice save," Jack said to Gale. "Was your card the Jack all along?"

"Of course," Gale replied as they continued through the crowd.

"Is the Nightingale really a European bird?" Jack asked.

"Yeah, I think so."

"Why weren't you named after an American animal?"

"I don't know. Maybe it was a call for speed and flight. If so, it worked because the Great Spirit made me able to run like a bird can fly."

They finally made it to the boat entrance where there were several men sitting behind a table. "May I help you boys?" one of the men asked.

"We're here to enter the Hearts tournament," Jack said.

"Well you're in luck. There are five spots left in the field of sixty-four. Do you have the entry fee?"

Both Jack and Gale pulled out the cash from their pockets and handed it over.

"Splendid!" the man said. "I'll say you're just about the youngest ones on the boat, but there's no age limit, so welcome aboard! We cast off at four o'clock this afternoon. Dinner is at six, followed by a reading of the official rules. Play starts at seven tomorrow morning. Head up the stairs to the second floor where you'll find the main desk, and they'll show you to your room. Good luck to you boys. There are some serious players on board, so you'll likely need it!"

They walked with their horses across a ramp that led onto the boat. Jack kept walking, but Gale stopped in the middle of the ramp. He turned back to look at the dock with all of the merchants and tourists, and he felt some trepidation about the new, unknown environment he was entering. But he steadied himself and walked ahead, knowing that courage was not the absence of fear but rather the will to press onward in spite of it. ♣

ale took one look at his room and gasped in amazement. This was upper-class living at its finest. The bed was enormous, and the pillows were the biggest and fluffiest he had ever seen. And it was all his, for Jack was in the room next door.

They changed into their new evening clothes (Hickok had insisted on paying for a trip to the tailor before the boys left town) and then descended the grand staircase in the middle of the boat. When they arrived on the second floor, they heard the steamboat whistle and felt the boat start to move through the muddy water. They quickly ran outside onto the deck and watched the shore as it slowly drifted away.

They walked back inside to the central room. It was big and open, and there were card tables everywhere. As people were milling about and socializing, Jack and Gale saw a crowd gathered in the corner of the room, and they walked over to see what was happening. The onlookers were watching two men of different ages play chess. The younger man appeared dashing and confident, while the older man had a more serious disposition. Judging by the pieces on the board, the latter was having a rough time of it.

"Wow, I think that's Paul Morphy," Jack said, wide-eyed.

"Who's that?" asked Gale.

Jack pointed to the younger man. "I can't believe it. He's the best chess player in the world, the best there's ever been. He went overseas and embarrassed the Europeans. He doesn't just win—he wins with style. Like at the Opera House in Paris, when he defeated two Dukes with a brilliant Queen sacrifice."

Morphy heard Jack's commentary and looked up with a smile. Then he flicked his head toward the board as if to say, "Watch this." The next three moves were pure Morphy—stylish sacrifices setting up a brilliant checkmate. The beaten man merely nodded his head and shook Morphy's hand, and the small crowd clapped in appreciation. Morphy tipped his cap and stood up, and he gave Jack a wink as he walked away.

"How do you know all this?" Gale asked. "Do you play chess?"

"Yeah, I love chess. Not that great at it, but I can play a little bit. Sometimes they reprint Morphy's games in the newspaper. I've seen his portrait illustrated there—that's how I knew it was him. I wonder if he's here to play Hearts."

They spent the next hour wandering around the ship and taking in the scene. Everyone they saw was older than they were, so they kept to themselves. Around five-thirty they headed over to the dining room where there were sixteen tables with four seats each—one for each of the sixty-four participants. In the front of the room, there was a large head table for the captain and the tournament administrators. Each table had name cards, and they found their names at a table near the back of the room.

Gale and Jack sat down with their backs to the wall and with a full view of the room. They looked at the other people with curiosity as they tried to get a handle on their competitors. The typical player seemed to be in his thirties or forties, well dressed, confident, and carrying a gun. A few were younger men or old-timers, and there were a few scruffier types that looked as though they had recently popped out of the saloon. Not too many women, though there were a few.

To Gale's eye, two people stood out. One was a gentleman with a sharp white suit and a large moustache. As he puffed on a cigar, he seemed to be having a great time regaling his tablemates with stories.

The second man was a dark, tall man with broad shoulders and chiseled features—the type of person one noticed when entering a room. He carried himself with complete confidence and was stylishly dressed, and there was no mistaking the two revolvers he wore at his side.

"Not sure what you got me into," Gale said to Jack.

"Don't worry. If you lose, at least you'll be losing Hickok's money," Jack said.

"But it was my money once he gave it to me. That was way more money than I'd ever seen in my life. I should've taken it and ridden for the hills."

Jack chuckled and then turned to see a man in his early sixties approach the table and sit down. Less than a minute later, a young girl came up and grabbed the fourth and final seat. She looked to be perhaps a year or two older than Jack, and he found himself momentarily breathless upon seeing her face. She was very pretty, with sparkling green eyes and ash blonde hair that fell to her shoulders.

"Looks like they stuck me at the kiddie table," the older man said.

"Funny, I was thinking the same thing," the girl echoed while looking directly at Jack.

"Kiddie table, huh?" Jack said with amusement. "Well, you could always switch with him over there." He pointed to a fellow sitting next to a three-toothed, scary-looking man.

"Well fine, then, I guess I'll be safe with the kiddies. Hi, I'm Celine," she said as she extended her arm. She spoke English well but had a slight European accent that Jack couldn't quite place.

"I'm Jack. Good to meet you."

"Who's your friend? Does he talk?"

Jack looked over at Gale. "This is Nightingale. Gale for short."

Gale put his left hand over his heart and stuck his right hand in the air. "How, white girl. Me Injun boy. Me hungry."

Both Celine and the older man had startled expressions before Jack interrupted with laughter. "He's messing with you!"

Celine looked at the boys with amusement and bewilderment. "So where did you come from? I'm very curious to hear how the two of you ended up on this boat."

Jack briefly explained how they met in the desert and then crossed paths with Wild Bill Hickok.

"Wild Bill Hickok?" Celine said. "I'd say that's ridiculous, but you couldn't make up a story like that if you tried."

"Where are you from?" Jack asked Celine.

"I come from New Glarus, Wisconsin. It's named after Glarus, Switzerland, where my family is from."

"Switzerland? Are you an alpine mountain climber?"

"No, we don't have any mountains in Wisconsin. I've never even been to Switzerland."

"So how'd you end up on this boat?"

"I needed to get away, and I'm quite the Hearts player, so what better way to have a little adventure?"

"You just better hope you don't end up at my table," Jack said with a smile.

The conversation was interrupted by the ringing of a bell, followed by a loud, bellowing voice. "Attention, everyone! I'm Captain Huxfield. Welcome to my ship."

The idle chatter in the room dwindled, and everyone turned to face the captain.

"You're here because you're either a great cardplayer, you have a lot of money, or both. Either way, I'm glad you're here. Some of you I've seen before, some of you I haven't. But I know that this year's tournament will be another fine one, the best Hearts tournament in the world. So we're going to start things off with some dinner— a glorious feast of venison, sweet potato, and cranberry sauce— and then Jonathan, the tournament director, is going to read the rules of the tournament. So have a good dinner and enjoy the ride!" There was a round of applause, but the room fell abruptly silent as a woman walked into the dining room through the double doors.

Whoa, Gale thought. *That's one way to make an entrance.* He'd never seen anyone like this woman before. She was strikingly beautiful yet exhibited a cold, dark aura. Her hair was long and black, her skin was fair, and above her dark eyes were slanting eyebrows. But it was her outfit that really stood out. She wore a fancy, royal gown and an abundance of jewels, and she carried a three-foot tall scepter with a giant emerald in the center. To top it off, she was adorned with a large golden crown. She looked out of place, like she was from another era. Following her was a young servant boy to whom she paid no attention.

"Ah, Queen Brunhilde, so nice to see you again," Captain Huxfield said. "Back to defend your title, I see!"

The woman looked contemptuously at the captain, saying nothing. She walked right past him and found her place at the one table with an empty chair.

Gale and Jack looked at each other with perplexed expressions. "Who is *that*?" Jack wondered aloud.

"That's the Queen," the other man at the table said. "I'm Harold, by the way. Nice to meet you young kids."

"Nice to meet you too, Harold," Celine said. "The Queen, what is she the Queen of?"

"Rumor has it she runs a slave island in the Caribbean. A tough woman."

"So why does she come all the way up here?" Jack asked.

"Hearts is her passion. She says it's in her blood. She's been coming here the last four years and has won every time. I was at her table two years ago. Very intimidating. I had the feeling that if I played the wrong card or did something to displease her, she'd take out a knife and stab me. Doesn't smile at all. Mean spirited and unpleasant, but she knows how to play cards."

Gale shook his head. "I definitely should've kept my money," he muttered. ♣

 he meal was served, and it was delicious. Neither Gale nor Jack had ever tasted such good food. While they ate, they talked about some of the people in the room.

"Harold," Gale said, "who's the man sitting over there?" He pointed to the first distinguished gentleman he had noticed earlier.

"Oh, that's Samuel Clemens," Harold said. "He's an aspiring writer. Boy does he know how to tell a story. Not much of a cardplayer though."

"And how about him?" Now he pointed to the second person he noticed—the tall, handsome man who at present was regaling a large group with a story. The men in the group were laughing, and the women in the group were looking longingly at the storyteller.

"I don't know who that is. Never seen him before. Looks like a charming fellow."

"How many years have you been here, Harold?" Jack asked.

"This is my fourth year. I've made it to the second round twice. One of those times was when I lost to the Queen."

"Do you have any advice for us?"

"Play your game," Harold said. "Don't be afraid of what others think or say. That's why the Queen wins. She intimidates people and then they make mistakes."

"And what's your strategy?" Jack said to Celine.

"Win," she answered, smiling.

"Great, I'll keep that in mind."

The dessert came out next, and it was warm apple pie with buttercream. Like the dinner, it was amazing.

While they were enjoying the apple pie, Jonathan got up from his table to address the room. "I want to welcome you all to the tenth annual Big River Hearts Tournament! For those of you who don't know me, I'm Jonathan Francis, President of the International Hearts Society and head administrator of this competition. You've made this the finest Hearts tournament and, dare I say, the finest card tournament in the world. Now the war is over—great news. That means we won't have to worry about getting caught in a battle zone this year."

After a brief applause from the players, Jonathan continued. "At this time I'd like to go over the schedule and official rules. There are sixty-four of you, and you've been divided randomly into sixteen tables of four. Pairings will be posted up on the wall here once I'm done talking. The first round starts tomorrow morning at seven, game score to 70. The sixteen winners move on to the second round where there'll be four tables of four, and that will start at one o'clock, game to 75. The four winners make it to the final, which starts at six o'clock in the evening, game to 100.

He then went on to explain the rules, and they were the same rules that Jack had explained to Gale in the Dry Gulch Saloon. "Let's keep the table talk to a minimum. And remember, it's expected that everyone adhere to respectable standards of gamesmanship and common decency. As it is, we have some, shall I say, younger entrants this year," he said while looking over at Gale and Jack's table.

"The winner of the tournament gets $10,000," Jonathan continued. "Second place gets $5,000. The rest of the entry fees go to this fine captain and crew and help pay for the great meals you'll enjoy. The money is in the safe behind me. The only person who knows the combination is Richard, our banker in New Orleans. He'll open the safe and give the winners the money when we arrive on Sunday. In the meantime, should there be any trouble whatsoever, Jackson here will get involved, and trust me, you don't want Jackson to get involved." He pointed to a very tall, muscular man standing in the corner. The man was scowling and had a long scar down his cheek.

"So with that, I'll say good luck and may the best player win! Is this the year the Queen's reign ends?" He laughed at his little joke but stopped when he looked at the Queen, who was not amused in the slightest.

"Let's go check out the matchups!" Jack said. He and Gale got up and walked behind the head table where the draw hung. They found their names on opposite sides of the large paper.

"I don't know anyone in my group," Jack said. "What about you?"

"The only name I recognize is that Samuel Clemens who Harold mentioned," Gale said. Gale turned around and looked up to see the tall, charming man whom Harold had not known looking down at him.

The man smiled and extended his hand. "Joe Kingman. Pleasure to meet you."

"I'm Nightingale, and this is Jack," Gale said as he shook the man's hand.

"Good luck to you boys," the man said, and then he walked past them to look at the pairings. Gale and Jack headed back to their table. Harold had left but Celine was still sitting there.

"Well, good night Celine," Jack said.

"Going to bed so soon?" Celine asked.

"Yes, I'm going to get a good night's sleep. I need to be at my best tomorrow."

"All right then. Maybe I'll see you at the tables."

"Yes, perhaps you will," Jack said with a grin. The boys rose from the table and were heading out of the dining room when they walked by the Queen's table. They both halted in their tracks, for she was staring at them with a look of pure hatred. Gale looked at Jack and said, "Come on," snapping Jack out of his temporary haze. They headed straight up to their respective rooms where the anticipation of the next day's events could not prevent them from falling right to sleep. ♣

ale woke up with a start. He lit a candle and glanced at the clock in his room which read five-thirty. Soon it would be time for breakfast, and then play would begin at seven. He had been a little nervous when first coming onto the boat, but now his nerves were dissipating. For what did he have to lose other than money that was not really his? He was a total newcomer to the game and was playing against adults, all of whom were likely experienced players. *Just enjoy the boat ride and good food,* he told himself.

He stepped out onto the deck and looked toward the east at the rising sun. It was a beautiful morning, cool and crisp. There were no clouds in the dark sky, which was starting to lighten up. As the ship slowly sailed southward, he could see land about one hundred meters off the port bow.

He looked to his left and saw Celine gazing eastward as well. He walked up to her and wished her good morning.

"Good morning Nightingale," she replied. "Did you have a good night's rest?"

"Yes, it was a very nice, warm bed."

"Where's your friend?"

"I don't know. Probably still asleep."

"So what's your story, Nightingale? How did you end up here?"

"Honestly, I don't know what I'm doing here. I just live day by day, and this tournament seemed like a good idea at the time."

"Do you have any family?"

"No, my parents are dead," he said. "I'm the last of my people. The only one left."

"Oh no, I'm so sorry!" Celine said with compassion. She paused, and then added, "I'm an orphan too."

"Really?"

"Yes, my parents and many others in my town died of consumption last year. I left before it could get me too. Now I'm doing what you're doing: living day by day."

"What made you decide to play here?"

"We played Hearts all the time in my town. I was the best player. I heard about this riverboat tournament and thought it sounded like fun. I borrowed the money to enter so I really need to win or get second."

"Well, that means you'll have to reckon with the Queen."

"There appear to be a lot of good players on board, but I'm confident in myself. I've been playing my whole life."

"You sound like Jack. He talked about playing all his life too."

"Jack, huh? I hope I get a shot at Mr. Jack," she said with a smile.

"We should go wake him up," said Gale.

They headed down to Jack's room. As Gale lifted his fist to knock, the door opened up, and Jack was standing there dressed and ready to go.

"Good morning!" Jack said. "Time to show these pros how we do it in Neffs, Pennsylvania."

"Neffs, schmeffs," Celine said mockingly. "If there were some more players here from my hometown of New Glarus, one of us would win for sure."

"All right, that's enough out of you, Swiss Miss," Jack said, laughing.

Gale just shook his head—would he have to listen to these two carry on during the whole trip?

They ate a quick breakfast and then entered the main room which was buzzing with activity. People were milling about, and the energy and excitement in the air was palpable. At the stroke of seven, a bell rang, and Captain Huxfield appeared.

"All right, everyone, find your name card and take your seats. The time to play cards has begun!" ♣

ale found his table and sat down. He was paired with Clem-ens and a husband and wife, the Halleys. Clemens was to his left, Mrs. Halley sat across, and Mr. Halley was to his right. In Hearts there are no strict rules against teamwork, and teams of-ten shift fluidly depending on who is in the lead—two players might work together on one hand but not on the next. But a husband and wife at the same table? That could be tough to overcome.

"Random draw, huh?" Clemens said to Gale. "About as random as the tax bill I get every year." Gale looked at the Halleys and saw them smiling back at him, as if they were saying, "One of us is moving on, and there's nothing you can do about it."

Clemens leaned over and whispered to Gale, "Don't worry kid, we can take 'em." He offered his hand for Gale to shake.

"Yes sir, Mr. Clemens."

"Tell you what, kid," Clemens said. "As long as we're on this beautiful boat, you can call me Mark Twain."

The game began, and fortunately for Gale, the cards were dealt in his favor. He knew from playing poker that the Card Gods liked to deal in streaks. Either it would be a hot streak, when the player magically receives everything he wants, or it would be a cold streak, when every hand is more miserable than the last.

Right out of the gate, he was hot. His cards were continually low, and he was deep in spades every time. He did not get the Jack of Diamonds on any of the first four hands, but he had hardly taken a trick, and he tallied two minus 5 point hands, one zero score, and one hand where he took two hearts.

And on the fifth hand, he got lucky. He was dealt the Jack of Diamonds, and when Twain led with the 4 of Diamonds, neither of the Halleys protected with the Ace, King, or Queen. That left Gale with a free Johnny, and he earned a minus 10 on the hand.

Afterward, Gale was sitting very pretty with minus 18, and he hardly felt as though he had done anything to deserve it. Twain was at 35, Mrs. Halley was at 40, and Mr. Halley was at 13. Now they were all teaming up to get Gale, trying to give him the Queen and getting Johnny Diamonds to one of the other three.

But even with their joining of forces, the other players were having a hard time sabotaging Gale. During one hand, Twain led the 4 of Clubs and Mrs. Halley threw the 5. Mr. Halley threw the Queen of Spades, thinking that Gale would have to eat it. But Gale happily threw the 3 of Clubs, and Mrs. Halley gave her husband a deathly glare. Then, during that same hand, Mrs. Halley led the 10 of Diamonds and Mr. Halley played the 8. Gale's only Diamond left was the Queen, and he was shocked when Twain played the Jack, thereby giving it to Gale. "My only Diamond," Twain said sadly.

When it rains good luck, it pours, Gale thought to himself.

On the final hand, Mrs. Halley sat at 65 and took a few early hearts which put her at 68. Twain led the 4 of Hearts, Mrs. Halley played the 5, and Mr. Halley dropped the 3. Predictably to everyone else at the rest of the table, Gale ducked with the 2. Mrs. Halley gave her husband another death stare, but she had no way of knowing that the 3 was his only heart. If he would have had a higher one, he would have played it to spare her some points and keep her alive. But she had busted, and with the Jack already having been claimed by Twain, the game was over, and Gale had won handily.

Mrs. Halley got up from the table without saying a word, and Mr. Halley followed after her. "I reckon he'll be sleeping on the floor the rest of the way to New Orleans," Twain noted.

"Between you and me," Twain continued, "I'm glad you whooped 'em. A husband and wife at the same table—I'm sure they thought one of them would win. But you showed 'em. Congratulations and good luck. Now I'm going to go and have a drink." He got up and patted Gale on the shoulder. As Twain was walking away from the table, Jonathan was approaching.

"So Mr. Nightingale, you're moving on. Congratulations, you're the youngest ever first-round winner! Next round's at one o'clock, and pairings will be up at twelve-thirty." Gale looked at his pocket watch. It was only eight-thirty! Most of the games were still going on. He looked around the noisy, crowded room. He spotted Jack, Celine, and Harold, all playing at separate tables. He did not see the Queen or Kingman—perhaps they had already finished their games.

He stepped outside to get some air. Now the sun was fully up and it felt warm. It was a gorgeous day and there was not a cloud in the sky as the steamboat plowed through the great, muddy river. There was a man sitting nearby playing the banjo, but there were not many other people on deck.

Gale stood against the railing and looked down at the water. *Whoa,* he thought to himself, *I'm in the second round.* He had not expected to win a game, let alone have it be that easy. He wondered whether he was actually a good player or if he was simply lucky. In poker, luck can win every now and then, but it is skill that triumphs in the long run. He guessed Hearts was the same way.

He had been standing and looking out across the river for about half an hour when he turned to hear a voice.

"Hey Gale, how'd it go?" Jack asked.

"I won. It was pretty easy. I got great cards the whole game. How'd you do?"

"I won too! Close game between me and one other guy. Going into the last hand, we were tied. One of the others busted on hearts, and the guy I was tied with got Johnny, but then I slipped him the Queen and beat him by a hair."

"Nice," Gale said.

"Hey, do you wanna sit over there?" Jack pointed to some deck chairs on the bow of the boat.

"Sure," Gale said.

"These are the best seats in the house," Jack said, sitting down and putting his feet up on the nearby table.

They sat in silence for a little while, enjoying the quiet and the view from the front of the boat.

"You know what's funny about this game," Gale finally said.

"What's that?"

"The Jack of Diamonds is the best card in the game. And that's my lucky card. Always has been."

"Really? Why's that?"

"Right here." Gale pulled out his Jack of Diamonds card from his pocket. "It's my lucky card, given to me by my mother." Gale handed it to Jack.

Jack took a quick look at the front, flipped it over, and was momentarily speechless. "Whoa," he finally uttered.

"What is it?" Gale asked curiously.

"This card, you got it from your mother? Where did she get it?"

"I don't know. She never told me. She just told me to always cherish and protect it. What's the problem?"

"It's not a problem—I just can't believe it."

"Can't believe what?"

Jack pulled out the Jack of Clubs from his pocket. "I have a matching one." ♣

Jack flipped his card over and held it next to Gale's. The backs of both cards were the same shade of royal blue, and both had a sword in the upper right corner and a shield in the lower left. On Gale's card, there was a white line across the middle, and above the line it said *High Street*. The back of Jack's card was identical, but instead the white lettering said *Low Street*.

"That's amazing," Gale said with astonishment. "They look the same. Where did you get yours?"

Jack was equally shocked. "I got it from my father who got it from his father. Like your mom, my dad told me to protect it and that it was good luck, and I've carried it around everywhere. That's all I know."

"I've always wondered what *High Street* is. I wonder if it's a real street somewhere."

"I've thought the same thing about *Low Street*. That's so strange. Two cards separated at birth. If only we knew where the rest of the deck was. I'll bet it's quite a story."

As they talked, Joe Kingman peered at them from around the corner. *Unbelievable,* he thought to himself.

And up on the second deck, the Queen stared down at them with great interest. *Should I move now?* she wondered. *No, be patient. Let it all play out.*

Jack and Gale put the cards back into their pockets. "Unreal," Jack said as they leaned back in their chairs and returned their gazes to the mighty river. ♣

fter a while, Celine came out looking dejected.

"How'd you do?" Jack asked.

Suddenly her pretend pout turned into a smile. "I won! Wasn't looking too good for me at first, but I rallied with some late Jack of Diamonds winners. Let's go have lunch and see if the new matchups are out."

They ate in the dining room and then headed back to the main room. Now there were only four tables left. Because most of the other tables had been folded up, the room appeared to be bigger. They walked over to the wall where the pairings were written. Jack looked up and turned to Celine with a big smile. "You and me, same table. It's on!"

"Come on now, you'll be nice to me, won't you?" Celine asked as she made puppy dog eyes at Jack.

"A wise man once said, 'Mercy is for the weak,'" Jack responded.

"Fine, then, if that's how it's going to be. Let's settle this once and for all!"

Gale looked up at his draw. Two of the players he didn't know, but the third was Morphy. "Hey Jack, I got Paul Morphy at my table."

"If he plays Hearts half as well as he plays chess, it could be a tough match for you. Did you know he plays blindfold chess with multiple boards?"

"Huh?" Gale said.

"Yeah, he gets in a room with multiple players, each one having their own board. They make a move, and then he makes a move by telling them what piece he's moving since he's blindfolded. Then he goes to the next board in a circle and plays up to fifteen people at a time. And he wins. His memory and intelligence are incredible." Gale looked over and saw Morphy across the room playing chess with someone else. He looked totally relaxed, as if he had not a care in the world.

"I don't know who I'd rather not face, Morphy or the Queen," Gale said.

"At least Morphy won't consider cutting out your heart if he loses," Jack retorted.

"Good point," Gale said.

Jonathan walked into the room and cleared his throat. "All right everyone, take your places. The second round is about to begin!" ♣

ale approached the table and sat down. Morphy was directly across from him and looking very suave and confident.
To Gale's left was a tall man named Dodson who looked
to be in his twenties. To his right was an elderly man, a Pole named
Janusz.

"Nice to meet you all," Morphy said warmly, and everyone at the
table shook hands. Some of the people who had lost the previous
round were milling about and watching the action unfold.

"Mr. Morphy," Janusz said with an accent, "I know you like to
give away your Queen on the chessboard. I hope you won't be so
generous with her at the Hearts table."

"I wouldn't dream of it," Morphy said with a laugh. Gale was
impressed—the man was just cool.

From the first deal of the cards, Gale could tell this was going to be
a different game from the last. The Card Gods were no longer on his

side; they must have decided he was having too much good fortune. He was dealt only one spade, the 8. He had two clubs and multiple diamonds and hearts. He decided to pass the two clubs to try to void himself of the suit so that if he got passed a bad spade, he could get rid of it quickly.

Unfortunately, Janusz gave him the worst possible pass: two clubs to replace the ones he had passed, and the Queen of Spades. With only two spades including the Queen, he was sure to eat it. Morphy won the first trick and then led with the Jack of Spades. Gale played his 8 and everyone else ducked the Jack. Morphy then led the 10 of Spades and Gale was forced to throw the Queen. He took a few hearts as well to end up with a score of 18 after the first hand. Morphy got the Jack and a few hearts to have a score of minus 7.

The next two hands were not much better. Gale did not get the Queen but ended up taking many hearts, and Janusz and Dodson both got hurt as well. Morphy was in total control, though he came back to earth a bit during the no-pass hand, which of all the hands is the most susceptible to luck. Morphy was dealt only two spades, including the Queen, which he had to eat.

The following round brought more of the same: an avalanche of points for Gale, Janusz, and Dodson, with Morphy playing the game like a Stradivarius. But once again Morphy got crushed on the no-pass hand. Even so, he had a good-sized lead, and after several more hands Dodson and Janusz were on the edge of death with 70 and 72 points, respectively, while Gale had 57 and Morphy had 35.

The next hand was another tough beat for Gale. Morphy kept leading spades, and eventually Janusz threw the Queen. Gale had multiple spades and could have ducked, but if he did that, Janusz would bust and Morphy would win. So he had to take the Queen with his King of Spades. He ended up getting Johnny to make things a little better, but he also took ten hearts to finish the hand at 70 points. Morphy still had 35, Dodson had 71, and Janusz had 74, one point away from busting.

Gale knew all three of them could not keep treading water like this, not when they all were so close to busting. The next hand, one of the three would get some hearts or the Queen and the game would be over. He had to go for a moon shot, no matter what his cards were. It was his only chance. ♣

By this point a crowd of about ten people had gathered around the table to watch, including Jonathan. The next hand was a pass right. Morphy finished dealing and Gale picked up his cards.

Clubs: K, 3
Diamonds: A, 2
Spades: Q, J, 9, 6, 5, 4, 3
Hearts: K, 10

He was long in one suit, spades, which was a good start for mooning. The low cards were bad, especially the 2 of Diamonds, because when diamonds are led, there is always the risk that the Jack will come out, and he needed the Jack to shoot the moon. The hearts he had were high, but not quite high enough—someone could beat them if he wanted to. Although the 3 of Clubs was a low card and not ideal, he could dump it on the first trick. He placed the 2 of Diamonds, the King of Hearts, and the 10 of Hearts face down on the table and passed them to Janusz.

The pass from Dodson was ready so he picked up the cards: the King of Spades, the Queen of Clubs, and the 3 of Diamonds. The first two were helpful, but the 3 of Diamonds was bad for the same reason as the 2 was. At least he had not been passed a low heart. Not an impossible hand, but he could be beaten with the Ace of Clubs, the Ace of Spades, and the Jack of Diamonds.

The hand broke down this way:

Gale:
Clubs: K, Q, 3
Diamonds: A, 3
Spades: K, Q, J, 9, 6, 5, 4, 3
Hearts: None

Dodson:
Clubs: A, J, 9, 8, 7, 5, 4
Diamonds: Q, 8
Spades: 10
Hearts: 9, 7, 4

Morphy:
Clubs: 10, 6
Diamonds: J, 7, 5, 4
Spades: A, 8
Hearts: Q, 6, 5, 3, 2

Janusz:
Clubs: 2
Diamonds: K, 10, 9, 6, 2
Spades: 7, 2
Hearts: A, K, J, 10, 8

Gale was not the only one thinking moon. Janusz had a strong hand with lots of high hearts, but there were also some low diamonds cluttering it up.

Janusz played the 2 of Clubs, Gale played the 3, Dodson threw the Ace, and Morphy played the 6. Gale was glad to see the Ace of Clubs gone, meaning that he had King and Queen high.

Dodson led the 4 of Clubs, Morphy followed with the 10, Janusz played the 2 of Diamonds, and Gale played the Queen. Gale was glad Janusz did not break hearts. Even though Gale would have taken the heart, an early break would mean that if another player led hearts for the rest of the game, Gale would lose the moon, and it was too early for him to win all the remaining tricks. Janusz was not breaking hearts because, unbeknownst to Gale, he was considering a lunar attempt of his own.

Now it was decision time for Gale: play the 3 of Diamonds, or run his spades out? Probably better to play the 3 of Diamonds, for if he ran his spades, he would still have to play the 3 eventually and then would lose out on the Jack. But if he played the 3 now, maybe it could go around the table without exposing the Jack. And even if Janusz laid the Jack, that wouldn't be the worst outcome. He threw the 3, which was followed by Dodson's 8 and Morphy's 7. Did Janusz have the Jack?

Nope. Janusz threw the 6, and Gale breathed a sigh of relief. Now all that was standing in the way of him and the moon was the Ace of Spades. Dodson then led the 10 of Spades, and Morphy followed with the Ace. An interesting play—was it Morphy's only spade, or was he fishing for the Queen in hopes of stopping a moon? Janusz played the 7, and now it was Gale's turn. It would have been easy to give Morphy the Queen, but there did not seem to be anything standing between him and the moon.

He paused for a moment, took a deep breath, and then threw the 3 of Spades. He looked up to see Morphy crack a smile of admiration for Gale's play. Like he had done so often in chess, Morphy had tried a dashing Queen sacrifice, but Gale had refrained from taking the bait.

Morphy followed with the 4 of Diamonds, Janusz played the 9, Gale threw the Ace, and Dodson played the Queen. Gale followed with the King of Spades and then led with the Jack of Spades, after which no one had any spades left. Gale's King of Clubs and remaining spades were all winners. He had shot the moon.

The group that was watching applauded with excitement. "Wow," Gale thought to himself. He had done it. He felt a shot of adrenaline course through his body, not unlike the feeling of winning a big poker hand. In fact, he had never felt this excited after winning a poker hand.

Gale chose to add 26 to everyone's score and subtracted 10 from his own, so the final tally was Janusz with 100, Dodson with 97, Morphy with 61, and Gale with 60. He had won by 1 point.

"Congratulations, young man," Morphy said extending his hand. "Good shoot," he said with a smile.

"Thanks," Gale said shaking Morphy's hand. The other two also congratulated Gale and then left the table.

"Mr. Nightingale," Jonathan said, "you're in the final! Do you realize how impressive this is? A fantastic achievement. And to beat the world chess champion—a job very well done!"

"Thank you," Gale said. It was good to win, but he was not about to get overconfident about it. He knew he was lucky—Morphy getting hurt on the no-pass hands, Janusz nearly busting out, and then the final moon shot and victory by a single point. But a win was a win, and he would not turn it down.

He got up and walked over to Jack's table. One of the other players was dealing the cards. "How'd you do Gale?" Jack asked. Gale flashed a thumbs-up sign.

"You won? That's great!" Jack exclaimed. Celine looked up and gave him a half-hearted smile. "Don't mind her," Jack said. "She's a little sore since she's been a dumping ground for my Queen. Maybe she was expecting some special treatment, but I was just showing her how we do things in Neffs." Celine responded with an evil eye to end all evil eyes.

Gale watched the next few hands in admiration. Jack was in control and finished things off with a minus 10, while Celine was stuck with plus 26—the worst hand of all.

"Good game everyone!" Jack said while shaking hands with the other players.

"I'm not shaking your hand," Celine muttered defiantly.

"No worries, just don't stay mad at me forever," Jack said with his incessant charm. At that moment, Celine wished she could take that charm and throw it into the river.

"We're in the finals, can you believe it?" Jack said to Gale.

"No, I really can't."

"I wonder who we'll be playing." The other tables were already cleared out. Whoever the winners of the other two games were, they had done it quickly.

Jonathan was standing nearby. "It'll be you two versus Kingman and the Queen at six o'clock tonight. You boys have been playing great, but the Queen—she's in another league. You'll need all your wits to even have a chance."

"I'll be rooting for the Queen," Celine said with a scowl.

"I'm going to unwind on the deck," Gale said. "Wanna come?"

"Yeah, let's go relax a little, and then we can talk strategy," Jack said.

"Celine, when you're done sulking, feel free to join us!" And with that, the two new power players left the game room. The next time they returned, the stakes would never be higher. ♣

The boys sat down in the front of the boat and were silent for a while, just closing their eyes and enjoying the quiet. It was late afternoon, and the sun was still shining but starting to drift farther and farther away to the west.

Finally Gale spoke. "So, what do we do now?"

"I say we play straight up in the beginning," Jack replied. "Every man for himself. But if one of us gets to winning and the other is out of it, I say the one who's out of it tries to help the other. I don't mind so much if Kingman wins, but not the Queen. There's something wrong with her. Almost like she's evil."

"Sounds like a plan," Gale said.

"Don't let her intimidate you, either," Jack said. "She's got a deathly stare, and she froze me up last night. Now I'm ready for it, though. She won't get under my skin."

"I'm not afraid of her," Gale said.

After a while, Celine came out and sat next to them. "Uh-oh, no more strategy talk, Gale. The Queen's spy is here," Jack teased.

Celine gave Jack a sheepish look and said in a soft voice, "I'm sorry."

"What was that? I didn't quite hear you, Gale did you catch that?"

"You're terrible," Celine said. "Anyway, I'm sorry I said I'd root for the Queen. She seems like an awful person."

"It's OK, I forgive you," Jack said with a smile. "After all, you're not used to losing, so it was a new experience for you."

"And now I owe four hundred dollars that I don't have," she said glumly.

"Oh don't worry about that," Jack said. "Gale or I will be happy to pay off your debt once we win the big prize. We'll have more money than we know what to do with."

"You think you're going to beat the Queen? She hasn't lost in four years."

"Well, there's money for the first and second place finisher, and there's two of us, so I'd say odds are that one of us will walk away with a little cash."

"I'm sure everyone on the boat save the Queen will be in your corner, so you have that going for you."

After a while they went inside to have dinner: a well-cooked T-bone steak with fingerling potatoes, cinnamon raisin toast, and topped off with a decadent crème brûlée. It was another wonderful meal, but now both the boys were starting to have a case of the butterflies.

"How ya feelin'?" Jack asked Gale.

"A little nervous. I've never played cards with a hundred people watching me."

"Yeah, me neither," Jack said. "This is a little more high-stakes than what I'm used to back in Neffs."

They finished their dinner and walked into the game room. Kingman was already sitting at the table talking to a few ladies who were surrounding him.

"Ah, hello boys," Kingman said. "Welcome to the final table."

"Yeah, congratulations," Jack said, and they all shook hands.

"Impressive that two young kids made it to the final," Kingman said. "I don't suppose you'll be working together?"

"We wouldn't dream of it," Jack said.

"Of course not," Kingman remarked. "I understand the Queen is quite a player and has never lost here. Fortunately for me, I've never lost anywhere."

Great, Gale thought. *Another Hearts pro.*

It seemed as though everyone on the boat was crowded around the table to watch the game. It was a lively mood and people were chatting and drinking merrily.

But suddenly the room got quiet as the Queen made her entrance. She was still decked out in full royal regalia, and she walked slowly to the table closely followed by the young boy who was always by her side. She sat down, looked each player in the eye, and then turned to Jonathan and simply said, "I'm ready." ♣

The seats had been drawn randomly. To Gale's left sat Kingman, to his right was Jack, and the Queen was straight across. Kingman had the first deal, and as he dealt, Gale looked up to see the Queen glaring straight into his eyes. *What's her problem*, he wondered. *Why does she seem to hate us?*

The cards were dealt, and Gale picked his up. Not a great hand. Not many spades and a lot of high hearts: the Queen, Jack, 10, and 9. Not high enough to shoot the moon, but high enough to take 10 points or more. Despite his lack of spades, he decided the hearts posed the greatest threat to his hand, and he passed the Queen, Jack and Ten to Kingman.

Fortunately Jack did not pass him any high spades, and the hand was looking great. Unfortunately, however, Kingman had been dealt the Ace and King of Hearts to go along with the hearts that Gale had passed. It was an easy moon shoot, and his score now stood at minus 10 while everyone else had 26.

"That was terrible," the Queen exclaimed, looking right at Gale. "How could you be so stupid?" In Hearts, when someone shoots the moon, the other players often blame the person who passed to the moon shooter. If the passer had only given away a low heart, then there likely would have been no moon.

But the first priority when passing is to take care of one's self. It is often better for another player to shoot the moon and have three players have a bad hand than for the passer to be the only one with a bad hand. And Gale had no way of knowing that Kingman had the Ace and King of Hearts—it simply had been bad luck.

"Why don't you worry about your own cards?" Jack said.

"How dare you, you insolent wretch!" the Queen barked at Jack. Kingman, meanwhile, was grinning with delight.

"Now now, Brunhilde, settle down," Jonathan said. "It's a long game." He looked over at Jackson, the security man, as if to say, "Pay attention in case the Queen gets out of hand."

Gale looked down at the table and not at the Queen. What was he doing here, playing some brand new game for high stakes against these crazy characters straight out of a fairy tale?

He picked up the cards for his second hand. Suddenly his confidence had returned, for this was a great hand—he had eight spades including the Queen. He could try to save it for Kingman who was in the lead, even though a big part of him felt like giving the Queen to the Queen.

He did not have to wait long to make a decision. On the second trick, Kingman led the 5 of Clubs, the Queen played the 6, and Jack played the 4. Gale did not have any clubs and could throw the Queen right now if he wanted to. The conventional play would be to save it for Kingman. But he was not interested in being conventional, and he threw the Black Maria down on the table with a flick of his wrist.

The crowd gasped. The Queen stared for a moment in shock. Then she looked at him, her eyes burning with fire, and let out a shriek. "You idiot! Are you insane?"

"I'm not the crazy one around here," Gale said looking right at her. Now that he had played his card, he was starting to feel more comfortable. What did he have to be afraid of? There was some laughter in the room, including from Jack and Kingman.

The Queen was left momentarily speechless at Gale's flagrant disregard for normal Hearts etiquette. "I will get you," the Queen said. "Mark my words, I will get you."

Gale wondered if she meant during or after the game. Either way, he did not care. There were enough people on the boat that he felt safe, and he had nothing to lose as far as the card game was concerned. He would go after the Queen every chance he got. The second hand ended with Kingman winning the Jack, and thus building his lead even further.

The next hand was another bad one for everyone except Kingman. He had been blessed with many clubs, which were made stronger by the two clubs and a heart that Jack had passed across. He played his only loser, the heart, once they had been broken. The Queen and Jack both ducked, and it came around to Gale. He could have taken it, but then the rest of the tricks were likely his, and he did not want to be the only one with a bad hand. So he ducked too and Kingman went on to shoot the moon for the second time in three hands. The score was the Queen with 70, Jack with 56, Gale with 54, and Kingman with minus 28! He had nearly a one-hundred point lead over the Queen.

The Queen once again blamed Gale for everything. "I will destroy you, you little demon!" she screamed. "Do you understand me? I will destroy you!"

"Brunhilde, settle down!" Jonathan exclaimed. "Any more threatening outbursts from you and you'll be disqualified." Jackson uncrossed his arms and watched intently for any sign of trouble from the Queen.

Gale calmly stared back at her. One of the earliest lessons from his tribal elder was not to show discomfort or displeasure in the face of ridicule because that only makes one's enemies stronger with the knowledge that they are having an effect. The attitude not only sent a message to the Queen—it also made Gale feel more confident and relaxed.

"Hey everyone," Jonathan said, "Let's take a ten minute break and cool down a little."

"Really?" Kingman complained. "I'm hot right now. Let's keep playing."

Jonathan held firm. "Everyone be back in ten minutes."

The Queen got up and stormed out of the room. Gale walked out the other side, and Jack and Celine followed him onto the deck. By this time, dusk was settling in and it was cool out.

As Gale stared down at the river, Jack put his hand on Gale's shoulder. "Don't worry about her," he said. "She can't hurt you, not with all these people on board."

"She just tries to intimidate," Celine said. "That's probably how she's won all those years. People play scared of her. But oh, that was great when you gave her the Queen of Spades!"

Gale smiled. "Yeah, that felt good." He looked at Jack. "What should our strategy be now?" he asked.

Jack looked out across the water. "We could just keep hitting the

Queen. It sure would feel good, and then one of us would get second place."

heir plan worked beautifully. On four of the next five hands, either Jack or Gale had the Black Maria, and each time they successfully gave it to Kingman. The fifth hand, the Queen gave it to him. One time Kingman was going for the moon, but Jack foiled him by slipping Johnny to Gale, giving Kingman the dreaded plus 26. Just like that, Kingman's seemingly insurmountable lead had evaporated, along with his charm and good humor.

The tension in the room was palpable and growing with each hand. There were frequent gasps, oohs, and aahs among the crowd, and Celine stood behind Jack and anxiously bit her nails.

On they played until the score was just about dead even. Going into the no-pass hand, Kingman had 87, the Queen had 84, Jack had 96, and Gale had 88. This next hand was probably going to be the last. Gale and Jack looked at each other. No pass meant no help—it was every man and woman for themselves.

It was Gale's deal, and he asked the Queen to cut the deck. She did so while scowling at him with sheer disgust. He dealt the cards, which ended up like this:

Gale:
Clubs: A, K, 5
Diamonds: 8
Spades: Q, 10, 9, 2
Hearts: A, 10, 9, 6, 3

Kingman:
Clubs: 9, 6, 3, 2
Diamonds: J, 4, 3, 2
Spades: J, 8, 7
Hearts: J, 7

Queen:
Clubs: Q, J, 10, 4
Diamonds: 9, 6
Spades: A, 6, 5, 4
Hearts: K, 8, 4

Jack:
Clubs: 8, 7
Diamonds: A, K, Q, 10, 7, 5
Spades: K, 3
Hearts: Q, 5, 2

Gale's heart sank. He had the Queen of Spades and only three other spades to protect against her. It was not the worst deal, but combined with the other high hearts and high clubs, there was not a whole lot to like about this hand. Jack, on the other hand, was glad to see the high diamonds, but he was nervous about the King of Spades.

Kingman opened the fateful hand with the 2 of Clubs. The Queen played the Queen, Jack played the 8, and Gale took the trick with the King. Gale was relieved, for now he could get rid of his only diamond and then maybe have the opportunity to toss the Queen of Spades on a diamond lead. He led his 8 of Diamonds, Kingman played the 4, the Queen followed with the 6, and Jack played the 7, so Gale won the trick.

He had not expected to win the trick, though, and now he did not know what to lead. He wanted to keep the high club and the low club in order to have the option of getting the lead or getting off the lead, so he decided to play the 10 of Spades. Kingman followed with the Jack, the Queen played the 6, and Jack happily discarded the King of Spades.

Jack then led the 7 of Clubs, a fairly safe lead in the no-pass hand. Gale played the 5, Kingman threw the 9, and the Queen laid the 4. Kingman then tried to smoke out the Jezebel with the 8 of Spades, which was followed by the 5, the 3, and the 2. Kingman led Spades again, this time the 7. The Queen played the 4, Jack played his Queen of Hearts, and Gale won the trick with the 9 of Spades.

Gale took a few seconds to stop and think. There had been two tricks where everyone had played spades, and on that last trick three spades had been thrown, which totaled eleven spades played. He had the Queen, which meant there was only one more spade out there. He remembered Jack had played the King, but had the Ace been played? No, he was almost certain that the Ace had not been played. And Jack had no spades, so if he led with the Queen, either Kingman or the Queen would be forced to take in the Black Maria.

Even though he was fairly sure that the Ace was still out there, it was still nerve wracking to lead with the Jezebel. It had been a long day. What if he had miscounted?

Oh well, here goes nothing, he thought as he slowly flicked the card onto the table.

Several gasps were heard from the crowd. What was he doing? Was he trying to shoot the moon on a no pass? Was he crazy? But soon they realized he was not crazy at all, for after Kingman played the Jack of Hearts, but before Jack threw the 10 of Diamonds, the Queen was forced to lay the Ace of Spades. The crowd cheered while Jack and Kingman were stunned. What a move! The Queen did not look at anyone as she took the trick—she knew she had been beaten.

So the Queen had been vanquished, but there was still the matter of who was going to win the game. Now all that mattered were hearts and Johnny Diamonds. Whoever got Johnny likely got the game. After the Queen led the 9 of Diamonds, Jack played the Queen of Diamonds because he could not take the chance that Kingman had Johnny, which he did. Gale played the 10 of Hearts, and Kingman played the 3 of Diamonds instead of the Jack.

Jack took a chance by playing the Ace and King of Diamonds on his next two leads, and his gamble paid off, for he won Kingman's two diamonds, including Johnny himself. He also took in some hearts: the King and 8 from the Queen, and the Ace of Hearts and Ace of Clubs from Gale. Next he led the 2 of Hearts, and Kingman's 7 beat Gale's 3 and the Queen's 4. The Queen won the next two tricks with her high clubs, and then the game was over. Now it was simply a matter of counting the score.

As the suspense in the room reached a fever pitch, Jonathan tallied up the score and announced the results. "So here it is, the moment you've all been waiting for—the final score! It's Queen Brunhilde with 101, Mr. Kingman with 91, Mr. Porelli with 90, and in first place, Mr. Nightingale with 89. Congratulations Mr. Nightingale!" A cheer went up around the table and a round of applause broke out.

"You did it! You won!" Jack exclaimed and patted Gale on the back.

"And you got second!" Gale replied.

Kingman got up without a word and walked out of the room. The Queen was still staring down at the table. Then she brought her head up to look at Gale. She appeared deranged as she pulled out a dagger from her gown and slowly held it up. Then, she suddenly screamed and jumped up on her chair and then onto the table.

Fortunately for Gale, Jackson was standing behind the table between Gale and Jack. Right as the Queen pulled her arm back to strike, Jackson punched her squarely in the face. It was such a blow that she flew back off the table and was knocked unconscious. Her crown also went airborne and landed right in the hands of Celine.

The onlookers were stunned, and Gale was wide-eyed with shock. It had all happened so fast. Jackson looked at Gale. "Are you all right, son?" he asked.

Gale looked down at the motionless body of the Queen. "Yes, I'm all right. Thanks for stepping in."

Jackson then turned to Jack. "And are you OK?"

Jack was also in a bit of shock. "That was crazy. She's crazy."

"She won't be bothering you anymore," Jonathan said. "We'll lock her up in the cell below deck. Then we'll deal with her once we get to New Orleans and you've gotten your money and are on your way. You won't see her again. Jackson, take her away."

Jackson picked up the limp Queen and walked out of the room, while Jonathan picked up the dagger that still lay on the table. "I'll hang onto this," he said.

"Ladies and gentleman," Jonathan said in a louder voice so the entire room could hear, "your Big River Hearts champions for the year 1865: Mr. Nightingale and Mr. Porelli!" The crowd cheered, and Gale could not help but feel better than he had ever felt. The thrill of victory, the sense of accomplishment, the money he had won, and the friends he had made—it was the best night of his life. ♣

The ship came to a stop outside a small town where it was to spend the night tied to a dock. It was fairly quiet on board as most people had gone to sleep, although there were still some night owls having a few drinks at the bar in the game room. Gale and Jack were wide awake after the drama of the evening, so they and Celine were hanging out on the third deck overlooking the water wheel at the stern of the boat. The town was nearby, but there were few lights visible at this time of night.

"Celine, you look ridiculous," Jack said. Celine was wearing the Queen's crown, and it was a little too big for her, having slid down almost to her eyes.

"That's Queen Celine to you. As the new Queen, my first edict is to make you my servant boy. I'd like a cup of coffee, servant boy."

"I think you're forgetting who's got the money. In my world, money is power, and so I think you'll be getting me a cup of coffee."

"Your world? You mean the exciting, fast-paced world of Neffs, Pennsylvania?"

As the two of them went back and forth, Gale looked off into the distance. He was still trying to process and make sense of everything that had happened. How had he managed to beat all these older, experienced players when he had just learned the game a few days before? Was he a genius?

No, he told himself, he was lucky. The first game everything went his way. The second game he would have lost to Morphy if not for the no-pass hands. And the third game Kingman had been winning by 100 points.

But he also had played well. He never quit against Morphy and found a way to shoot the moon when he had to. He and Jack were able to hit Kingman hard when that was their only play. And he brilliantly exposed the Queen on the last hand.

He reached into his pocket and felt his Jack of Diamonds. If only his mother had been alive to see him now, how proud she would have been.

Eventually Jack and Celine got tired of arguing and they sat back and relaxed. "What are you going to do with your money?" Jack asked.

"I have no idea," Gale answered.

"Well, if you want to come to Neffs, you can stay with our family."

"Really? Thanks. I guess I'll have to think about where I go next."

Suddenly they heard loud noises and the sound of yelling coming from other parts of the boat. "What do you suppose that is?" Jack wondered aloud. Then they heard what sounded like a gunshot.

⚜

Jackson's lifeless body lay outside the cell. A young man put a pistol, still smoking, into his holster and then reached down to Jackson's belt and unhooked the keys. He unlocked the door and the Queen stepped into the light. Her crown was gone and her face was bruised.

"My God, mother, what did they do to you?" he asked. ♣

Jonathan and Captain Huxfield were sitting and talking in the captain's quarters when the Queen strode in followed by her son and five other men.

"Wait. How did you—" Jonathan started to say as he stood up.

The Queen pushed him back down into his chair and grabbed her dagger that was on the nearby table. "We're taking over," she said.

"Wait, wait, wait," Captain Huxfield stammered. "You can't do that! This is my ship!"

The Queen turned to her son and pointed to Jonathan. "This one we need alive, for he will get us the money when we get to New Orleans."

Then she pointed to the captain. "This one, we don't need," she stated. Her son pulled out his pistol and shot the captain through the chest.

Jonathan's eyes widened with horror. The Queen turned to one of her men and said, "Stay with him." To another, she ordered, "Start the cast-off. We leave for New Orleans tonight." Then she turned to her son. "Erik, let's spread out and find those kids. I'll go to their quarters. You search the rest of the ship. You know what to do." They turned and walked out of the room.

⚓

"Do you think we should head back to our rooms?" Celine asked.

Jack ran to the edge of the deck and saw ten armed men boarding the ship. "I don't have a good feeling about this," he said. He looked down at the water and noticed an attached boat, a small piroque. There was a rope extending up from the piroque that tied to a post next to them on the third deck.

Suddenly the door from the interior cabin opened. It was the young boy who was with the Queen.

"They're taking over the ship," he said.

"Who is?" Jack asked.

"All the Queen's men."

"Are you working for her?" Jack asked suspiciously.

"Not by choice," the boy replied. "I'm her slave. Since they captured her, I slipped away. I'm hiding and looking for a way to escape, but I think I waited too long. By the way, my name's Pierre."

The others quickly introduced themselves. "Well, you can stay with us," Jack said. "I think we need to get off the boat now."

"But what about your prize money?" Celine said. "You earned that money. You can't let her get it."

"Well we're in no position to take on the Queen's army," Jack replied. "That's a losing hand."

Then the door opened again, and a man walked forward with a gun.

"Hello, you little rats," he said.

"Who are you?" Jack asked.

"That's her son, Erik," Pierre said.

"Pierre, I'm disappointed in you. My mother's not going to be too happy when she sees the company you've been keeping."

"What do you want?" Jack said. "We don't have any money."

"You're right, you don't have any money, and you won't get any money. I heard about how you cheated my mother, the two of you working together," he said while looking over at Gale.

"Good insurance plan," Jack reasoned. "If she wins, she sails to New Orleans to collect her money. If she loses, you take over the ship. Still doesn't explain what you want with us."

"What I want is—"

Suddenly a shot rang out. Jack jumped back instinctively and then looked down at his body to see if he had been shot. He looked up and saw Erik fall forward face first, for someone had shot him in the back. A man stepped out of the shadows—Kingman.

"Oh, Mr. Kingman, thank you!" Celine said with relief. "You saved our lives! This man was going to kill us."

"It was the least I could do," Kingman said with a smile as he put his gun down.

"C'mon, let's gets out of here," Jack said while starting to walk away.

"Hold it right there," Kingman said. Jack turned around and saw that Kingman had re-raised his gun and was pointing it right at him.

"What do you want with us, Kingman?" Jack said.

"You don't need to call me that anymore," he said with a new Mexican accent. "You can now refer to me as the Coronado Kid." ♣

here were noises reverberating throughout the ship. People were moving about and it was only a matter of time before the Queen's men reached the third deck.

"Of course," Jack said. "Hickok said you liked to shoot the moon." Then he remembered his brother. "And you attacked the fort. What did you do with my brother?" Jack took a step forward.

The Kid still held the gun. "We don't have much time."

"Well, what do you want? We don't have our money yet."

"I'm not interested in your money."

"Well, what then?" Jack asked.

"Your cards."

"Our cards?" Jack said.

"Yes, your cards," the Kid said with a grimace. His smile had disappeared.

"What do you mean?" Jack asked.

"You were looking at them earlier today. You have a Jack of Clubs and a Jack of Diamonds," the Kid said, while Pierre had a look of surprise on his face.

Jack and Gale also were perplexed, and they looked at each other and then back at the Kid. "You're kidding, right?" Jack said.

He cocked the gun. "Nope."

"What would you possibly want with those?" Gale said.

"What are these cards he's talking about?" Celine asked.

"Hand them over," the Kid said.

"Mine's in my room," Gale said. "I'll have to go get it." He started walking away but the Kid waved the gun.

"No, no, no, I know you have it here."

Gale quickly ran over to the side of the boat and pulled the card out and held it over the water. "Let them all go," he said, "or I drop this card." He looked out at his card, dangling over the water. He would hate to part with it, but he had no choice.

"No!" the Kid screamed. He quickly pounced upon Jack and grabbed him, holding the gun to his head. "You drop that card and I kill him, right here, right now."

The sounds of commotion on the boat were getting louder. "You have ten seconds to give me those cards," the Kid ordered while briefly looking over his shoulder. "Ten. Nine."

Gale stepped away from the side of the boat and looked down at his card. It had been given to him by his mother and was his most valuable possession. He touched the Jack's face one final time and then gave it to the Kid. The Kid released Jack, and then Jack reached into his pocket and gave the Kid his card.

"Thank you boys, it's been a pleasure," the Kid said with a smile, his good humor having returned. He moved toward the cabin door, and as he was exiting, he added, "and if you see Hickok, tell him the Kid is riding again." And then he was gone.

Gale was stunned by the loss of his card. He had possessed it his entire life. "How did he know we had those cards?" Gale asked. "And why did he want them?"

Jack was equally shaken, especially after having had a gun pointed at his head. "I don't know," he said. "I don't get it."

"Are you all right, Jack?" Celine asked as she gave him a hug. "He could have killed you."

"Yeah, I'm OK."

"And I don't understand this card business. What just happened?"

Before anyone had a chance to respond, the door opened and they turned to see the Queen. She was holding her silver dagger and looking none too pleased. She glared at Celine who was still wearing her crown. The Queen took a step toward Celine, but then she looked down and saw her son's lifeless body. Her eyes filled with rage and she let out a visceral, primal scream.

"We didn't do it," Jack said while slowly backing up. "It was the Kid— I mean Kingman. He was just here. Honestly."

"How could you do this?" the Queen said. "HOW COULD YOU DO THIS?" She charged at Gale with the dagger. Jack quickly grabbed a lantern hanging overhead and threw it at her. The glass broke and her gown caught on fire. She fell to the ground and started screaming as her clothes began to burn.

"C'mon, we gotta get out of here!" Jack yelled as he grabbed the dagger that had fallen from the Queen's hand. He ran over to the side of the ship where the piroque was attached. The others followed, but first Pierre stopped by Erik's body and grabbed something from the inside pocket, and Celine took another lantern that was overhead.

"What about Raindrop?" Gale exclaimed.

"There's no time!" Jack countered, and with that they took turns climbing down the rope and into the piroque. Once they were all in, Jack cut the rope with the dagger, and he and Gale started to paddle.

Several of the Queen's men had heard the screams and came running onto the deck. One of them grabbed a nearby curtain which he used to stamp out the fire. The Queen was alive but her arms and legs were badly burned. "Forget me, go get those brats!" she ordered while pointing off into the distance. A few of the men ran toward the side of the ship and fired their guns at the distant piroque, but the kids were out of range.

"They're getting away," one of the men said.

"Well, go get them!" the Queen yelled.

Schmidt, a large blond German man and the Queen's top lieutenant, stepped to the forefront. "You five," he said pointing to several of them, "stay with the Queen. Everyone else, come with me." He led ten of the others down the steps and into two large rowboats tied to the ship. They jumped in and cast off immediately, chasing the smaller boat into the night. ♣

There were two oars in the piroque—Gale had the front and Jack had the back while Celine held the lantern. They heard the shots but knew they were far enough away to be out of range. Pierre pulled out his spyglass and saw the two boats in the distance. "They're coming after us," he said.

"Let's get off the river," Jack said. They turned off of the Mississippi River and into a tributary. The town quickly faded off into the distance as they got farther away from civilization.

"Can you see them?" Jack asked.

"I can't tell," Pierre said. "It's too dark."

The only light available was from the lantern and the moon overhead. The river had taken them into a forest, and before they knew it they were in the middle of a very dark swamp.

"I don't have a good feeling about this," Jack said.

"Where are we?" Celine asked.

"The bayou," Jack answered. "I've read about the bayou. It's a maze of swamps."

"And there are alligators," Pierre said.

They stopped paddling for a moment and just listened to the symphony of crickets that surrounded them.

"Well, we can't stay here and we can't turn around," Celine finally said.

"Might as well head north then," Gale said. He looked up through the trees at the stars. He found the Great Bear and the Little Bear, just like his mother taught him. At the end of the Little Bear's tail was Polaris, the North Star. "This way," he pointed.

They paddled for about half an hour through the dense marsh, not saying a word. Along the way they glimpsed several birds, bats, and two alligators. The gators were half above water with their eyes closed, but one of them opened an eye as the boat swam past.

They continued to paddle and eventually happened upon a small cabin in a clearing on the edge of the swamp. There were no lights on or signs of activity.

"You think someone lives here?" Celine asked.

"Doesn't look like anyone's home," Jack said. "Let's stop and see if there's any food. Maybe we could even hide out for a bit."

They docked the boat next to the cottage and got out. Once they reached the front door, Jack opened it slowly and held out the lantern. "Hello?" he called softly.

There was no reply. The cabin was dark but full of furniture. They walked in and looked around. There were shelves of canned food and meats by the window. "Perfect," Jack said, and he and Gale grabbed a few cans and gave them to Pierre to carry in his satchel.

Gale looked out the window and saw a light in the distance. "What's that?" he said.

Pierre looked through his spyglass. "It's a man fishing." Gale took the spyglass and had a look. He was sitting on the dock by himself alongside a lantern.

"Seems like an odd time to be fishing," Gale said.

"He must be an odd guy if he lives out here," Celine noted.

As Jack was grabbing more food, one of the shelves collapsed and about ten cans loudly crashed to the floor.

"What are you doing?" Celine whispered loudly.

"I didn't do it on purpose! The shelf just broke!" Jack said with frustration.

Gale looked back at the man through the spyglass. He had heard the noise and turned to look back at the cabin. Then he picked up a rifle and started walking toward them. At that moment they heard voices from the other direction. Gale ran over to the window on the other side and looked out. He did not need the spyglass to see that the two boats carrying the Queen's men had pulled up.

"They're here," Gale said. "We have about twenty seconds until they enter."

"There's a cellar," Jack said, pointing to a set of doors in the floor. They ran to the doors and pulled them open, and a musty smell wafted up from the dark hole. They quickly descended the steps and shut the door behind them. The doors were wooden, but there was a metal bar that served as a lock. Jack grabbed it and fitted it in the slots on either side of the doors.

"Someone went to a lot of trouble to build this basement on the edge of a swamp," Jack noted.

Celine was still carrying the lantern, and she quickly walked around the edge of the cellar. It was small and tight.

"There's nowhere to go," she said. "We're trapped." ♣

ack climbed the stairs and put his ear to the door. He heard many voices, including one with a high-pitched, Southern drawl. "Look what they'd done. I'll kill 'em! I'll kill 'em!"

"Do you live here?" a voice with a German accent asked.

"Yeah, just moved in las' month. Heard some noise no more 'an a minute ago and I came a-runnin'. They gotta be in here." Then he pointed to the cellar. "There, they gotta be there."

"Well, let's get them," the German man said.

"You can have 'em!" the fisherman said with glee.

"Stand back," one of the men said.

"Oh boy," Jack said as he jumped down the steps just as a shot rang out. He scampered to the edge of the room and turned around and looked back at the door. Several more shots rang out, and Jack felt his pulse quicken. The door had held, and a voice called out, "Get the axe."

Suddenly the axe started to strike the door at a furious pace. "We're in big trouble," Jack said.

Pierre reached down to the floor and picked up a dark blue scarf. "I don't believe it," he said. "This looks like my mother's."

"Why would your mother have been here?" Jack asked.

"I don't know," Pierre said. "It couldn't be hers. It looks just like it though."

"Was your mother a slave?" Jack asked. "Did she escape?"

"Yes."

"Then maybe this was an Underground Railroad station."

"Huh?" Gale said.

"This isn't the best time for a history lesson!" Celine stated.

Jack ignored her and lifted up a rug that uncovered a hard floor. "In order to get away, the slaves moved north along escape routes. They stopped at stations and were helped by conductors. Stations would have secret exits."

He looked at a small dresser against the wall. "Gale, help me move this," he said. They slid the dresser to the side to reveal a hole in the floor and a ladder that led down the hole.

"Here it is! Let's go." Pierre went first, followed by Celine and Gale. Jack went last but stopped after descending a few steps. He turned to look back up at the cellar. With all his might, he reached back up and pulled the dresser legs so that it covered the hole.

He covered it just in time, for the axe finally broke through and the men poured down the stairs. He could see them from under the dresser. The big, blond man looked around and screamed, "They're not here! Find them!"

As the men started running up the stairs, Jack climbed down the ladder to join the others. It was pitch black, and he lit a match to reveal a tunnel big enough to crawl through. "Let's go!" he whispered loudly, and they crawled for what seemed like a quarter mile. Eventually they got to the end of the tunnel and another ladder, this one much taller than the last.

They climbed to the top, arriving at what looked like a door. Gale opened the door and climbed out, and the others immediately followed. They were on top of a hill, and they were able to look down at the cabin which was still in view. There were men all over scouring the area.

"I think we've lost them!" Jack said. "Let's get out of here while we still can." He started walking and led the others over the side of the hill, out of the swamp, and into the forest that had just begun. ♣

The long war may have been over, but the Underground Railroad and its vestiges had not outlived their usefulness. They trekked through the night as Gale led the way along the trail with Polaris guiding the way in the northern sky. Gale had to slow down a little, for the others could not match his speed and endurance. The adrenaline had been pushing them, but it had been a long day and they were getting tired.

"What do you think about stopping soon?" Celine asked after they had traveled a fair distance.

"This looks like a good spot to make camp," Gale said. There was some space on the ground for the four of them to settle in while also being sheltered from the tall trees overhead.

Gale started to collect wood for the fire, and Celine and Pierre gathered leaves to make leaf beds. Jack took out the canned food stolen from the cabin and opened it with the Queen's dagger.

Jack then got out a match and lit the fire, and it gradually grew into a full burn. The four of them sat on logs around the fire, stuffing their faces with the canned meat and fruit. It felt good to finally relax, and they sat for a while, eating in silence.

"What a day," Celine finally said once everyone had finished eating. She was still wearing the Queen's crown. "The Queen's son, ready to kill us. And that awful Kingman. I knew we couldn't trust him. What did they want, anyway?"

"Our cards," Jack said, staring into the dancing embers.

"What's so special about your cards?" she asked.

"I don't know. I've had that Jack of Clubs my whole life. And we just discovered that Gale has a matching Jack of Diamonds."

"It was given to me by my mother," Gale said.

"What do you mean by 'matching'?" Celine asked.

"Same color, size, and symbols on the back. The only difference is that mine says *Low Street* on the back and Gale's says *High Street*."

"That's the craziest thing I've ever heard," Celine said. "What would the Queen or Kingman want with them?"

"I don't know," Jack said.

"It makes no sense," Gale added.

Pierre was sitting quietly but listening intently to the conversation. "Maybe they're Lost Kingdom cards," he interjected.

They all turned to Pierre. "What?" Jack asked.

"You know, the cards from the Lost Kingdom. Why else would the others want to take them?"

Gale and Jack exchanged puzzled glances. Gale turned back to Pierre. "What's the Lost Kingdom?" he asked.

Pierre sat himself up on the stump he had lain against. "Really, y'all have never heard the legend of the Lost Kingdom? In slave quarters, we tell stories over and over—it helps pass the time. Every slave south of the Mason-Dixon knows about the Lost Kingdom. You wanna hear about it?"

"Hmm, let me think a minute," Jack said sarcastically. "Uh, yeah, I would." Gale and Celine both nodded in agreement.

"All right then," Pierre said. "It's time to go way back in time to a land across the sea." He stared at the fire and began to tell a story. ♣

"To one and all, welcome to Borolessia on this beautiful day!" the town crier proclaimed to the gathering masses. "Thank you for attending the annual summit of kings. For those of you who have traveled a great distance to be here, thank you for your efforts. And most of all, thank you for your support, your dedication, and your loyalty to the finest kingdom in the world!"

The sun was shining upon the gleaming castle and the air was warm. It was a magnificent day. Thousands of citizens of Borolessia waited outside the castle in anticipation of the royal parade. Every year, the kings began their summit with a dramatic and lively parade, and it was a thrill for the commoners to see their heroes up close.

The buzzing crowd grew quiet when four trumpeters suddenly appeared on top of the castle and began playing a fanfare. Their long trumpets had large cloths hanging down that were adorned with their respective king's royal symbol.

"Look, Ma, it's starting!" a small peasant boy said, pointing toward the bend in the road where two great black horses were coming into view. They were pulling an open carriage that had a giant black club painted on each side.

The trumpets stopped as the crier called out, "Our first royal family comes from Italia, the land of Caesar, fine wine, and olives. Please welcome King Francesco, Queen Giovanna, and young Giuseppe! King Francesco—the King of Clubs!"

King Francesco stood up, smiled, and waved to the people. He was an older man with white hair, but he was distinguished and muscular. He was so named because he came from a long line of great warriors, and the club was their weapon of choice. He was a good-hearted king and preferred not to rule with an iron fist, but in this feudal age of knights and castles, sometimes the club was mightier than the quill.

He encouraged his wife to stand up next to him. She was younger than the king and very beautiful. She got up and blew several kisses to the crowd as the people continued to cheer.

Behind the carriage, Prince Giuseppe was riding on a large steed. He was a happy eleven-year-old who liked to be outside and run around, and he was not fully aware that being a prince made him different from the other kids. But today he was a prince, and he smiled and waved just like his parents did.

Behind him were several floats that were evocative of Italia, and they included men dressed as ancient Romans and women throwing grapes and olives into the crowd.

After the Italians had processed, the crier stepped back up to address the people. "And next, coming all the way from España, home of bullfighting and siestas, say hola to King Javier, Queen Elena, and Prince Enrique! King Javier—the King of Hearts!"

The king and queen were both in their early sixties. King Javier came from a long line of kings who were famous for having multiple queens, and it was not until he met Queen Elena that he settled down into a monogamous relationship. On this day, they smiled and waved to the crowd atop their white horses which wore black garments with bright red hearts sewn into them.

The prince, meanwhile, was continuing the family tradition of being a ladies man. As he rode past the crowd, women squealed and some even fell faint. Not only was he a wealthy, powerful prince, but he was also devastatingly handsome. And being in his mid-twenties, he was at the perfect age to receive admiration from women both older and younger than he.

He smiled as he thought of the night ahead. While the four kings were having their executive summit, there would be a grand royal reception in the castle. To close the summit, the kings would address the gathered with a State of the Kingdom report. The guests were important people from throughout the kingdom including dukes, earls, and barons. There would also be royal duchesses, who would be throwing themselves at him with the dream of one day becoming a princess, and he could have his pick of the litter. Such was the life of a young, handsome, single prince.

There was one thing, though, that he loved more than women, and that was money. No one save one other individual knew the extent of the young prince's devotion to wealth.

After the España floats went by with señors and señoras wearing colorful costumes, the crier stepped up once again. "I know you'll give a warm welcome to our esteemed royals from Britannia. From the land of dragons, dark forests, and magicians, it's King Harold Wellington, Queen Violet, and Prince Curtis! King Harold—the King of Diamonds!"

A mighty cheer went up as the tan coach carrying the king and queen approached the castle. Like King Javier, King Harold was in his sixties. He was a rotund fellow with a gray beard and a warm disposition. He went nowhere without his axe, which was strapped to his back. Queen Violet was in her fifties and wore a beautiful necklace made out of diamonds. The king owned many diamonds, including a stash so valuable that it was rumored to be the greatest treasure in the world.

Behind them rode Curtis, the Jack of Diamonds. He had turned eighteen last month and, like the Jack of Hearts, was handsome and sure to be a target of the ladies at the royal ball. Unlike Prince Enrique, Curtis was shy and not quite sure of himself around women. He was not fond of being the center of attention, but he gave the crowd a smile nonetheless as he looked down on them with his brilliant blue eyes. He carried a great shield that was red and blue with golden trim and displayed a bird slaying a dragon.

The cheers were loudest for the final king, the one who was hosting the meeting this year and therefore had the most support from the home crowd. "Ladies and gentlemen," the crier enthusiastically announced, "please put your hands together for your king and the king of Germania. From right here in Borolessia! Say hello to King Ludwig, Queen Ingrid, and young Princess Kiersten! King Ludwig—the King of Spades!"

The crowd went crazy with admiration for the Teutonic king. He was a legendary figure in these parts, having started as a peasant farmer with a simple spade and finishing as the king who united Germany. He was old and in ill health, but he mustered up the strength necessary to lead the summit and to do his part as the host king.

Next to him was Queen Ingrid, the Queen of Spades. She was a young woman in her early thirties, strikingly beautiful, but cold and frosty. She loved the power and the riches that royal life brought, but she was tired of being on the outside looking in at the four kings. Her ambition to rule the entire kingdom was unrivaled. She smiled and waved to the crowd while holding on to her large scepter, a brilliant piece of craftsmanship with a green emerald in the middle.

Behind them rode Princess Kiersten, their twelve-year-old child. She basked in the attention from the people while wearing a fake smile. Kiersten was capable of charm and pleasantry, but she knew how to manipulate and lie from an early age.

The king's family entered the castle, built on a great hill and over-looking the Baltic Sea. From this point on, access to the inside was by invitation only. King Ludwig descended from his carriage and greeted the other three kings who had been waiting for him. They had not seen each other in a year, and they were all genuinely happy to renew acquaintances.

"Ludwig, fine sir. Good show!" King Harold said as he extended an arm. Ludwig bypassed the arm and gave the King of Diamonds a full hug.

"Ah, Javier, nice to see you!" the King of Clubs exclaimed.

"And you as well, Francesco!"

Their relationships went back seventeen years, to when they had fewer gray hairs between them. At the time, Europe was in chaos. The continent was under siege from marauders from the East, pirates from the South, and rebels from right at home. Each king had his own set of difficulties, and it was King Harold who thought there was strength in numbers, so he sent an invitation to the other three powerful kings to meet him in London.

The kings were initially suspicious of their rivals, but that suspicion melted away quickly once they got to know each other. They discovered that if they allied together and supported each other militarily and economically, their united strength would be far greater than as individuals. At the core of their relationship was trust, for if one king got greedy, it could be trouble for all of them. But after almost twenty years, there were no conflicts between them, and life in their united kingdom was as prosperous and peaceful as it had ever been.

"Come on," Francesco said. "Let's go talk through our problems, like what to do about the French!" The four kings walked out of the courtyard and into the castle where they alone would hole up in a room and discuss the current state of the kingdom. ♣

While the kings discussed the affairs of state, the royal reception was taking place in the grand hall of the castle. Evening had set in, and the moonlight shone through the magnificent stained glass windows and into the large room where members of the four royal families were holding court. They mingled freely with the royalty of Europe, nobles of less prestige but no less ego and ambition.

As a trumpeter and harpist entertained with song, servants walked around offering the guests plates of food which featured a choice of boar or reindeer in addition to rosemary potatoes, plum pudding, and the king's own maple-brewed beer. Flags from across the kingdom lined the hall, and in the middle there flew four large flags adorned with the symbols of the kings: the Club, the Diamond, the Heart, and the Spade, with the Spade being the biggest and grandest of all.

At a table in the corner, the Jack of Diamonds was sitting and eating by himself while surveying the scene. He saw Giuseppe, the young

Jack of Clubs, approach him with some food of his own.

"Hi Prince Curtis, nice to see you! Mind if I join you?" Giuseppe asked.

"Absolutely! Good to see you too, Beppe. How have you been?"

Giuseppe smiled with a youthful vigor. "I'm doing just fine! I like these trips where I get to travel with my mother and father. I don't like having to dress up but I do love eating dessert." Curtis laughed at Beppe's multiple goblets of plum pudding.

"Is there anyone here your age?" Curtis asked.

"There's Princess Kiersten. I remember two years ago we had a great time playing together, but last year she ignored me, like she was too good for me."

"Speak of the devil," Curtis said as young Kiersten walked by. She glanced over at the princes and gave them a haughty smile. She did not say a word as she turned her glance away from them and kept walking toward a table of older boys whom she joined and immediately became the center of attention.

"I don't know what her problem is," Giuseppe said. "She used to be so nice."

"Sometimes people change when they get older," Curtis said. "She's getting to be more like her mother every year."

"Speaking of the crazy lady, I haven't seen her yet," Giuseppe said.

Curtis looked around the room. "Hmm, I guess I haven't seen Queen Ingrid either." He had noticed Prince Enrique in the opposite corner of the room surrounded by a dozen other women. They were literally waiting in line to get their turn to have an individual moment with the prince. They used this time as a sales pitch of sorts, for if they could successfully flirt with the prince and capture his attention, maybe they would stand a chance at becoming his princess one day.

One of the women waiting in line turned to look at Prince Curtis. "What about him?" she said to the damsel next to her.

"The Jack of Diamonds?" the damsel replied. "He's a quiet one. Really awkward."

"Does he have money?" the first one asked rhetorically. She smiled and tossed her hair. "Maybe I can get him to break out of his shell!" she said as she got out of line and walked across the room.

"Good luck!" the damsel said.

Across the room, Prince Curtis saw the woman approaching. "Oh dear," he muttered.

"What's the problem, don't you like women?" Beppe asked.

"I like women, but most of these ladies aren't my type. And I'm not good at the kind of idle chatter that ends up happening at these parties."

"What is your type?"

Curtis looked over at a young woman across the room. She was wearing a blue veil and had long, golden hair. She was sitting by herself and looked to be focused on eating her food.

"There," he said pointing at the woman.

"That's Princess Daphne!" Beppe said.

"You know her?" Curtis asked, a little surprised.

"Her father is an influential French noble. He came to Rome with her last year. She was very nice. A little more of the quiet type."

"Just like me," Curtis said.

Daphne looked up from her food and noticed the two princes looking in her direction. She smiled at them, and Curtis felt his heart mildly flutter. He smiled back and was tempted to get up and approach her when the other woman reached their table and sat down next to them.

"Prince Curtis, it's so nice to finally meet you, I've heard so many things about you! I'm Duchess Jones from Wales. I've seen you from afar, but you are much more handsome up close." The Duchess was wearing a red gown to match her red hair and had a big nose and a grating voice.

"Nice to meet you too, Duchess," Curtis said unenthusiastically. There followed a few seconds of silence.

"You really are the quiet type, aren't you?" the Duchess said as she placed her hand on his thigh. "Why don't you come back to my table and we can get to know each other a little better?"

Curtis stood up quickly. "Uh, sorry Duchess, but Giuseppe and I were just about to go outside and play a game of jacks. Isn't that right, Beppe?"

"Uh, yes, that's right. Come on Curtis, let's play that game we were, uh, just talking about."

They both got up and left the Duchess cursing at them under her breath. Curtis looked over to Princess Daphne's table and saw her looking at him. He gave her an awkward smile and she smiled back, and then he and Giuseppe walked out of the ballroom.

Meanwhile, Prince Enrique was still holding court with his numerous admirers when he caught the eye of Queen Ingrid from across the room. She looked at him and flicked her head toward the door.

"Excuse me ladies, I must leave for a moment. But don't worry. The prince will return!" he said as he left the group. He walked outside the ballroom into the hallway and continued a few paces until suddenly one of the doors opened and an arm pulled him inside.

Queen Ingrid and the prince were all alone, and they shared a lengthy, passionate kiss. Unbeknownst to anyone else, they had begun an affair at the previous year's meeting in Rome. The Queen was actually closer in age to the prince than she was to her own husband. Like many royal marriages, hers was an arranged union motivated by political gain, not love. She had a wandering eye and no qualms about using her power and beauty to get what she wanted.

They finished their kiss, but the Queen still held her arms around the prince's neck. She took a breath and looked him in the eye. "The time is ours. The time is now. Are you ready?" she asked.

He sighed. "It is a big step we're taking, but I am ready," he said.

"Good," she said with a smile. "The kings are finishing up their meeting now. Before they address the crowd, the four families are gathering in the chapel. I called for a prayer. That will be in about fifteen minutes. Get ready."

"I'm ready," he said. He kissed her and then left the room.

The Queen went over to the mirror in the corner and looked at herself. She held her head up and adjusted her ornate, golden crown. Soon it would be her kingdom. Not just Germania, but all of Europe. It would all belong to her. She had waited so long for this moment.

Fifteen minutes later, she exited the room and headed for the chapel. On the way, she passed Schultz, the lead general of the Borolessia army and the king's personal bodyguard. She nodded to him and he nodded back.

When she arrived at the chapel, she was greeted by her three fellow queens. The chapel was small and held no more than twenty-five people at a time. Minutes later, the four kings appeared along with Princes Curtis and Giuseppe.

"Ah, Queen Ingrid, so nice to see you!" King Francesco said. "And to call a time for us to gather in prayer, what a lovely idea."

"I didn't remember you as the most devout member of the group" King Harold said to the Queen. The Queen smiled but said nothing.

"She's not," King Ludwig said. "I don't know what's gotten into her. Maybe she's been indulging in my private beer collection." The other kings shared a laugh. The Queen looked around for Prince Enrique but he was nowhere to be seen. *Where was he?*

She was concerned that he might backtrack at the last possible minute. But that would not stop her plan. She had no need for him and his spinelessness. She would make him pay for not publicly supporting her, but that could come later.

The Queen moved to the center of the room. "Thank you everyone for coming here tonight and making time for something important to me—giving thanks to our Lord and Creator." Curtis furrowed his brow with surprise at the Queen's uncharacteristic behavior.

The Queen continued and said, "Form a circle around me, join hands, and bow your heads." The royals did as they were told.

"Dearest God, we thank You for the blessings You have reigned upon us. We put our trust in You that You may give us the wisdom, the vision, and the determination to do what is right for us and our people.

"A good leader has the courage to make difficult decisions even when others may not agree. A good leader has the strength to make weaker subjects succumb to his will. Germania's power has been reduced. Her wealth diminishes as nobles grow haughty and rebellious.

Meanwhile, she subordinates her power and her independence to a council of foreign rulers that doesn't have her best interests at heart. I'm talking, of course, about all of you."

Everyone stopped holding hands and exchanged bewildered glances over the Queen's surprising soliloquy. King Ludwig was the most astonished of all at the Queen's boldness. "Ingrid, what's the matter with you? Have you lost your mind?"

"You know," she said turning to face him, "I really should have done this a long time ago." She walked up to him, removing her dagger from its sheath, and stabbed King Ludwig in the heart.

"Ingrid," he said softly as he fell to the ground.

A state of shock fell over the room. There were gasps at the sight of the king dying, but everyone was too stunned to say anything. Giuseppe's eyes widened with fear, and Curtis instinctively put his arm around him to protect him. The King of Clubs ran over to the dying king and cradled his head as he exhaled his last breath.

Finally the King of Diamonds broke the silence. "My god, Ingrid! What have you done?" he said as he put his hands on his head in disbelief.

Ingrid stared at him with piercing eyes. "You're the one who got us into this mess. You and your vision of a united Europe. King Harold gets to live out his dream while the rest of us disregard our own desires and abdicate our decision making powers!"

"What mess?" the king responded with emotion. "Europe has been as peaceful and prosperous as it's ever been!"

"Maybe your Europe has, but from this moment, your Europe no longer exists," she said, looking at everyone in the room. "Now it's my Europe." Schultz walked in along with seven German knights all wielding swords.

"What are you going to do? Kill us all?" the King of Clubs asked.

"Not yet," the Queen said with a smile.

"Well, what do you want then?"

"Your cards. I need your cards." ♣

During the kings' initial meeting seventeen years ago at King Harold's round table, the host king needed to prove to the others that he could be trusted. Rival rulers do not naturally tend toward cooperation, and a show of good faith was necessary if Harold was to convince the others that unity was worthwhile.

He had decided to share with them the source of his great wealth—his vast diamond treasure. The diamonds were of the finest quality and were said to be so large and numerous that their value was almost priceless. He gave the other kings one diamond each, but there was more to his gift.

"My nephew, Edward, is quite the artist," King Harold said. "He created some pictures with your likenesses on them—he calls them cards. Show them, Edward!"

A thirteen-year old-boy walked into the room and stood next to the round table where the kings were seated. He was small and thin with light brown hair, dimpled cheeks, and a nasal voice. He showed little emotion as he held up his set of cards for the kings to see.

"I made one card for each week of the year," he said. "Four suits in all, to represent the seasons of the year and also the four of you. Each suit has numbers from one to ten, and I called the one an Ace. Then there is a Jack, a Queen, and finally, the King."

The kings smiled at this young and precocious boy. "Edward is a sharp young lad!" the King of Diamonds remarked, "I've asked him to devise a way to give you access to my treasure while keeping it safe from outsiders. What he has come up with is quite ingenious!"

The boy searched through his set until he found the four cards he was looking for. "At the king's request, I have hidden his diamond treasure. On the back of each Jack is one clue to its location. I have coated the cards with a special sealant to make them long-lasting and resistant to the elements."

He passed out the Jacks to the four kings. "To King Francesco, I give you the Jack of Clubs. To King Javier, the Jack of Hearts. To King Ludwig, the Jack of Spades. And finally, to Uncle Harold, the Jack of Diamonds."

King Harold smiled. "Thank you, Edward. I can assure you all that I don't know what is on the back of your cards or what Edward has done with my diamonds. The fewer people who know where they are hidden, the better. Now we all have a stake in the kingdom, and we're in it together. Most of us have more riches than most people could ever dream of, but if we ever face financial hardship, we can use the diamonds as a last resort. But only if we all agree. Edward says that each card's clue is necessary in order to find the treasure."

"King Harold, this is very generous of you," King Francesco said. "And you, young man," he said turning to Edward. "You are a clever boy!"

"Thank you, sir." Edward shuffled his remaining forty-eight cards and held them out to King Francesco. "Pick a card, but don't show me what it is."

King Harold laughed. "Edward is an aspiring magician. He enjoys trying out the little tricks he devises!"

"All right, I pick this one," Francesco said. He looked at the card and then showed the 2 of Clubs to the other kings.

"Now put it back in the pile," Edward said. He shuffled the cards and then laid them face down on the table. He moved his hand across the deck and stopped in the middle.

"Your card is here," he said, reaching down and turning the card over to show the 2 of Clubs.

"Bravissimo! How did you do that?" King Francesco asked.

"I cannot say," Edward said with a stone face. He collected his cards and walked out of the room.

King Harold shook his head. "He takes his magic very seriously, that boy."

⚔

"I'll start with you," the Queen of Spades said to the King of Diamonds. "Let's have it." King Harold looked at his wife and then over at his son. He reached for his axe, at which point the knights in the room took several steps forward.

"Relax," he said. He sighed as he put his hand around the blade and removed it from the handle. He put the handle on the ground and then tilted the blade with one hand so that a card fell out into his other hand.

He handed it to the Queen. She looked at the back of it and was pleased. She pulled out her own card and admired them side by side.

"You won't get away with this," King Harold said. "My people will never submit to you."

"Nor mine," the King of Clubs echoed.

"They won't have a choice," the Queen said. "I've called in all the armies of Germania. They've arrived in Borolessia and are awaiting my orders. My military is stronger than all of yours put together. It's time that we stop taking orders and start giving them."

She turned to the King of Hearts. "Your turn."

King Javier reached into his robe, pulled out his Jack of Hearts and handed it to Ingrid. "You despicable woman," he said with disdain.

"Funny," the Queen laughed, "that's not what you told me that night in Madrid." She turned to look at Queen Elena. "Yes, it was a magical night. He told me how dissatisfied he was."

The King of Hearts pulled a dagger from behind his crown and charged at the Queen of Spades. "Die, evil woman!" he yelled.

Schultz quickly intercepted the king from the side, stabbing him through the heart with his sword. "You first," the Queen said to the mortally wounded king as he fell to the ground.

The Queen of Hearts looked up at Ingrid with rage. Elena grabbed her husband's dagger from the ground and threw it at her rival, but Ingrid leaned back and successfully dodged it. She turned to Schultz and said, "Kill her too." Schultz did as he was told, and the King and Queen of Hearts were no more.

"Oh my God!" the Queen of Diamonds said in horror. The Queen of Clubs put her head in her hands, sobbing.

"So, that leaves one more card," Ingrid said, turning to the King of Clubs. "Let's have it." The King of Clubs remained silent.

The Queen approached him with dagger in hand and held it an inch away from his throat. "The card. Now."

King Francesco looked over at Giuseppe, who was still being protected by Prince Curtis, and nodded. The Queen looked over her shoulder at Giuseppe and barked, "Grab the boy!"

Giuseppe ran toward the chapel wall and threw himself through the stained glass window. He landed on his side and then quickly jumped to his feet and started to run. Four of the knights followed through the window while the other three went out the door.

The Queen remained and turned to the King of Clubs. "Whether or not we catch your boy, you can tell me what's on the back of that card."

The king looked back at her with stone-faced silence.

"This is the first time I've seen you at a loss for words," the Queen remarked. But still the king said nothing.

"I can make him talk," Schultz said, stepping closer to Queen Giovanna and pulling out his sword.

"Wait, Schultz. There's time for that later," Ingrid said. "First let's work on getting the boy back. Then he can watch his parents die." She flashed an evil grin at the King and Queen of Clubs.

One of the knights returned to the chapel. "He got away," the knight said. The Queen surveyed the chapel, plotting her next move. "Take them out of here," she said to Schultz. "Lock them up in the dungeon down below. Except that one." She turned to the Jack of Diamonds. "A hanging in the castle courtyard will show the people who's in charge now. Let's start with him." ♣

iuseppe ran as hard as he could until he found himself in the central courtyard. The royal party had recently ended but there were still people milling about. He stopped for a second to look down at his arms. There were a few scratches but nothing serious. He turned around and saw four knights about twenty meters away in hot pursuit. He started running again but knew that he was not fast enough to get away—they were going to catch him.

Suddenly a black horse carrying a cloaked rider came from behind and pulled up next to him. "Get on!" the rider called out, extending an arm. Giuseppe did as he was told and grabbed the rider's arm. He pulled himself up onto the back of the horse as the rider furiously charged toward the castle exit. The two guards who were standing on the drawbridge were facing the other direction, and by the time they turned around to see the horse coming at them, it was too late. The guards leapt out of the way of the charging horse and into the moat.

The horse continued down the hill away from the sea and into the valley. They had ridden about five minutes when the rider stopped at a clearing. There were no trees on this part of the hill, but there were large boulders that provided some cover. The rider dismounted, removed the cloak, and extended a hand to Giuseppe. Giuseppe looked up at the rider, and the moonlight revealed the long, golden hair of Princess Daphne.

"Princess Daphne, thank you!" the boy said, giving her a hug.

"It's good to see you, Giuseppe," the princess said. "Are you all right?" She squatted down to look him in the eye.

"Yes, I'm OK. A few scratches but I'll live. How did you know to come rescue me?"

"Because I have magical powers," the princess said proudly.

"Really?"

The princess shook her head. "No, not really. I was getting ready to leave. I don't really like parties, and this one wasn't much fun. I saw you being chased by those knights and figured you were in trouble."

"You figured right. I was in big trouble."

"What happened? Why were they after you?"

"A lot has changed in the last hour." He proceeded to tell Daphne about the events in the chapel and the card he held in his possession.

"Oh my goodness, that's awful! I never had a good feeling about that Queen," Daphne said solemnly.

"What are we going to do? She'll kill my parents if I don't bring that card back. And then she'll probably kill them anyway."

Suddenly they heard a horse galloping toward them, and they quickly ducked behind a nearby boulder. The horse stopped a few meters away, and the knight dismounted while scanning the countryside. Giuseppe looked at Daphne with fearful eyes, and she put her arm around him.

A moment later the knight walked around the rock and stared down at them. "Ah, just what I was looking for. The Queen will be so pleased with me!" the knight boasted.

"Excuse me, good sir?" a voice called out. The knight turned around to see an old man walking down the hill. He seemed to appear out of nowhere. He was of average height but was slumped over and used a cane. He had long white hair and a nasal voice. "I'm looking for the castle. I hear there's a party tonight."

The knight laughed. "I think you missed the party, old man." The knight turned back to Daphne and Giuseppe.

The old man persisted and approached closer. "Please, sir, take me to the castle."

Now the knight was annoyed. "Look, old man..."

He turned around and saw the old man's cane seconds before it struck his head. The knight took the blow but stayed on his feet. He charged the old man, but the old man was too quick, unleashing a series of moves that dropped the knight with ease. Daphne and Giuseppe looked down at the motionless knight, and then up at the old man. Giuseppe cowered in fear, and Daphne remained huddled over him.

"You don't have to be afraid," the man said.

"Who are you?" the Princess asked.

The man stood up straight and removed a wig to reveal a short crop of light brown hair. "My name's Edward. I'm on your side." ♣

32

Giuseppe looked up with awe. "You mean Edward the Magician? Nephew of King Harold and creator of the cards?"

"Yes, that's me." He held up his right hand and then quickly closed and reopened it to show a gold coin. He gave the coin to Giuseppe who was impressed by the sleight of hand.

"You're a legend! Prince Curtis told me all about you, but I wasn't sure if you were real. Hardly anyone has ever seen you."

"I keep a low profile. There are a lot of unsavory people out there who wouldn't mind finding out some of my secrets, like the location of the royal treasure."

"The royal treasure?" Daphne asked.

"A vast storehouse of great wealth. It started with King Harold, who pledged his diamond treasure as a sign of trust and an insurance policy for the kingdom. Each of the other kings has contributed to it with their own riches over the years, but none of them knows where it is. Only me."

"Unless they all agree to bring their four cards together," Giuseppe said.

"Yes," Edward responded.

"Well, the Queen of Spades has three of them," Giuseppe said.

"And the fourth?" Edward asked.

Giuseppe reached into his pocket and pulled out his Jack of Clubs.

Edward breathed a sigh of relief. "Good boy," he said with approval.

"Forgive me for asking, Sir Edward," Daphne said, "but if your knowledge is so valuable, aren't you taking a tremendous risk by being here?"

Edward nodded. "Yes, it's very dangerous. My uncle wouldn't want me within one thousand miles of here."

"Then why?" Daphne asked.

"Intuition. I've lived my life in the shadows. The last few years I've traveled across Europe. Always in disguise, I've kept my eyes and ears open, getting a pulse on the movements of armies and the ever-changing winds of power.

"I'd been hearing through various channels about a plot involving Queen Ingrid. I had no proof, but I began to suspect she was up to something. I was there in the shadows at the conference last year in Rome, and I slipped in and out of Germania this year looking for clues. But I hadn't been able to get close enough to figure out what she was up to."

"So you thought something bad might happen at this year's meeting?" Daphne said.

"Yes," Edward said. "I know the king wouldn't want me here. If I were caught, I don't think they'd ever break me, but I can't say that for certain. All I know is that if the Queen ever got a hold of that treasure, there would be no stopping her. She'd control Europe for generations. It was a risk I had to take."

"Well, lucky for us you got here when you did," Giuseppe said.

"So what are you going to do next?" Daphne asked.

"Rescue my cousin, Prince Curtis."

"Can't you just do some magic? I heard you're the best there is," Giuseppe said.

"Unfortunately it doesn't work like that," he said. "We're going to need more than a magic trick."

"What are they going to do to him?" Daphne asked.

"I've just come from the castle courtyard. They're talking of a hanging at the crack of dawn."

"Oh no!" Giuseppe said, putting his head in his hands.

Daphne was equally concerned. "What are we going to do?" she asked.

"I have an idea, but I could use some help," Edward said.

"I'm in," Giuseppe said. "After we get Prince Curtis, can we get my parents too?"

"Of course," Edward said.

"I'm in too," Daphne said.

"What's your idea?" Giuseppe said with anticipation.

Edward pointed to the fallen knight still lying on the ground. "It involves a little help from our friend." ♣

The morning had arrived, and the wind was blowing gently. The sun was peeking up over the horizon, and there were some deer grazing in a meadow outside the castle walls. Inside the castle, the Queen looked down from a balcony at the crowded square. This was her time, her moment. She did not say anything to the gathering crowd—she simply stood there, holding her scepter.

Around the courtyard there were knights stationed at several places, and in the middle there was a scaffold. Word had begun to trickle out of the castle and had reached the people: Queen Ingrid was going to be the queen of Europe, and she was showing off her newfound power by executing Prince Curtis at dawn for crimes against the state—her state.

A drummer started to play, and Prince Curtis was led out of the castle and into the courtyard. His hands were bound, though his arm still held his great shield. He looked around at the mass of people. Some were jeering at him while others were silent. Were they all going to willingly support the Queen? *Didn't matter,* he reflected, *as long as she ruled with an iron fist.*

Curtis turned his head and looked up at the Queen. She returned his glance with one of disdain. He was walked up the steps and into the noose. *It ends here,* he thought to himself. *At least it was a good eighteen years.* The sounds in the courtyard died away, and the floor dropped. ♣

as it all a dream? As he lay on the ground gasping for breath, a knight pulled him from under the gallows. He and the knight then jumped onto the back of a horse. There were several explosions and people screaming. The horse was galloping furiously, racing past the guards and across the drawbridge. The sun was up and shining brightly, the air was cool and crisp, and the birds were singing. This could not be real. It had happened so fast. Was this heaven?

He held on to the knight as they rode through the forest down toward the sea. When they reached the sand, the knight dismounted and extended a hand to the prince. Curtis got down and then looked at the knight. "Are you here to take me to heaven?" he asked.

The knight took off the helmet, revealing the beautiful face of Princess Daphne. "Not today!" she said with a smile.

"Daphne!" the prince said with a bit of shock. He looked around at the beach and the ocean. "I'm alive," he said in a moment of realization. "I'm really alive."

He looked back up at her smiling face. She was even lovelier up close. Maybe this was heaven after all.

"Thank you," he said to her. He extended his hand, but she skipped the handshake and instead put her arms around him and gave him a warm embrace.

"What happened back there?" he asked when they finally separated.

"I rode in as a knight," Daphne explained. "I snuck under the gallows where I waited until you fell, and then I grabbed you and we rode like the wind on the back of Eve here. It's the second time in twelve hours that I've saved a prince riding through the courtyard on this horse!"

"How did you just grab me? What of the rope?"

"Giuseppe was on the castle rampart with a special mirror, one that creates a powerful beam of light from the sun. Fortunately the sun was out today. He aimed it at the rope and the light beam burned through it just in time."

Curtis looked up at the sun and saw it disappear behind a cloud. "Fortunately indeed. No wonder my neck is sore," he said while shaking his head out. "Now what of this magic mirror? And the explosions I heard?"

"Your cousin Edward was also on the rampart, and he fired flaming arrows at the two large stashes of gunpowder in the courtyard. That created the chaos which aided our escape. And he gave Giuseppe the mirror. He's quite the wizard, I hear."

Curtis's eyes widened. "Edward's here? I don't believe it."

Daphne nodded. "It's true. We should keep moving, and then we can talk some more."

They got back on the horse and rode a short distance to a cave that was on the edge of the beach overlooking the water. Daphne tethered Eve along some nearby rocks, and then she and Curtis climbed up to the cave. They had a beautiful view of the ocean, and the sound of the crashing waves was calming.

"Where are they now?" Curtis asked once they had sat down.

"Edward had a horse ready. He and Giuseppe should be here any minute now—as long as they didn't run into any trouble."

"He's a brave kid," Curtis said of Giuseppe. "The way he jumped through the chapel's window. Without him, all would likely be lost."

He looked up at Daphne. "And without you, of course. How did you end up getting involved in this?"

Daphne gazed out to the sea. "My father is not well. I came here to represent our small duchy. The French barons can't agree on anything, except that they want no part of your father's kingdom."

Curtis smiled. "Yes, France has been the one area that has resisted being part of our united Europe."

"Yes," Daphne said. "My father and I always believed in your father's vision. We tried to get the others on board, but they were loath to relinquish their independence. And perhaps, with yesterday's events, they were right."

Curtis shook his head. "I never trusted that woman. King Ludwig was a good man, but she always seemed like she was up to something. Clearly she was. To see her murder her husband like it was nothing, and the King and Queen of Hearts too. I wouldn't have thought her capable of that."

"Do you think she can be stopped?" Daphne asked.

"Ludwig's army, now hers, was the finest fighting force in the world. If we don't rescue my father and King Francesco, there will be no one to check her. They are the only ones who have the credibility to reach the people, to make the masses believe that this united kingdom meant something."

"What about you?" Daphne said. "You could lead the people."

Curtis blushed. "Thanks, Daphne, but I'm not ready yet."

"How are we going to get them out?" she asked.

"I don't know. I'm sure the Queen will increase the number of guards now that I've escaped. It'll be a fortress."

"But now we have four, rather than just three," a voice said at the opening of the cave. Curtis turned to see Edward standing there with Giuseppe beside him.

"Edward!" Curtis ran over and embraced his cousin. "It's great to see you. And you," he said, turning to Giuseppe, "thank you for coming to rescue me."

Giuseppe smiled. "It was all Daphne," he said. "The Princess rescuing the Prince!"

Curtis chuckled. "Yes, I suppose so. Edward, I still can't believe it's you. What are you doing here? And where have you been the last few years?"

"Around Europe," Edward responded. "In and out of the shadows. I can't stay in one place too long or I risk getting caught, so I'm constantly on the move."

"What are we going to do?" Curtis asked. "We need to get my parents out. His too," he said, pointing to Giuseppe.

"First we need to rest," Edward said. "Then we strike at night. I have a plan."

As Curtis and Giuseppe built a fire, Edward looked out into the distance. The skies over the distant ocean had clouded up, and bolts of lightning regularly lit up the sky. "Winds from the north," Edward said. "That storm is coming our way."

The fire was now built and the four weary travelers lay around it, each one lost in his or her own thoughts and thinking about the night ahead. The rain had started and the thunder was getting louder. "I suggest we get some rest," Edward said. And with that, they all closed their eyes and drifted off to sleep. ♣

hey slept amidst the pouring rain and the booming thunder. Curtis awoke with a flash, not unlike the flash of lightning that had just pulsated through the atmosphere. He sat up and saw Daphne and Giuseppe still asleep, but Edward was sitting at the cave's entrance, watching the storm which had shrouded the day in darkness.

Curtis walked up and sat alongside him. "It is good to see you, cousin," he said, putting a hand on Edward's shoulder.

Edward nodded. "Yes, it is good to see you too."

"You know it's really dangerous for you to be here."

"I'm sure your father will agree," Edward said. "And you're right. The fact is, I can't stay away when there are bad things happening to my family and to the kingdom."

"Well, it's good you were here. You saved my life."

"Beppe and the princess played a part too. The little kid told me he had good aim, and he was right."

"So what's the plan going forward?" Curtis wondered.

Edward looked off into the distance. "A ship is coming here later tonight to take us back to London. I've arranged it with the captain, who owes me a favor. I'd like Daphne to meet the ship and tie one end of a long, thin rope to the bow," Edward pointed at a large rope that was in the corner of the cave.

"Meanwhile," he continued, "the three of us will ride to the castle with the rest of the rope. I'll get inside and then you and I will scale the wall and secure the other end of the rope to the castle. Giuseppe will ride back to the ship, and we'll go get your parents and fly out of here."

"I thought of one problem," Curtis said. "They're in a locked cell, and only the Queen of Spades has the key."

Edward shook his head. "Not a problem."

"How so?"

He pulled out a key. "A special key I created that unlocks nineteen locks out of twenty. That's a ninety-five percent chance that it'll work."

"And if it doesn't?" Curtis asked.

"Then it's on to plan B," Edward responded.

"Which is?"

Edward shrugged. "What we'll make up if plan A doesn't work."

"And what about this rope of which you speak?" Curtis asked.

"I got the rope and two oxen to carry it from a friendly farmer who lives nearby. The oxen are presently resting a few meters inland under some trees."

They slept on and off until the night arrived. As the rain continued to fall outside, Curtis went over to the fire and removed one of the pine logs. He let it cool for a few minutes, and then he took a knife and scraped off some of the tar that had formed on the surface. Giuseppe awoke to see him spreading it along his cheeks in multiple lines.

"What are you doing, Curtis?" he asked.

Curtis's normally light-hearted disposition had vanished and was replaced by a fervent focus and seriousness. "I'm going to do whatever it takes to save our parents."

"Can I have some of that too?" Giuseppe said.

Curtis passed him the log, and Beppe began to apply the war paint in the same manner as the elder prince whom he admired in so many ways.

Edward walked over and motioned toward the sleeping Daphne. "Let's wake her up," he said. "The time to strike is now." ♣

They started the short trip up the mountain. Edward walked in front of the large grey oxen to help guide them through the trees, and Curtis and Giuseppe followed behind, unraveling the rope along the way. Curtis turned to see Daphne standing at the water's edge holding the rope's other end. The rain was pouring down, but she was standing there in the moonlight watching them move farther and farther away.

They climbed up the rocky hill through the forest, with each step drawing them closer to the danger that awaited them. Eventually they arrived at the forest's edge near the western end of the castle, which was about one hundred meters away, and they saw guards everywhere on patrol.

"She's got the whole army here!" Giuseppe exclaimed.

"She knows we're coming," Curtis noted.

"So what are we doing with this rope anyway?" Giuseppe asked.

"Ever hear of a zip line?" Edward said.

"No, what's that?"

"Daphne's going to tie her end of the rope to the ship when it arrives. We're going to tie this end to the top of the castle. Then we're going to slide down the rope at lightning speed while hanging on to these." Edward opened a pack he was carrying and pulled out a metal bar bent at a forty-five degree angle.

"That sounds fantastic! I get to do that, right?" Giuseppe asked.

"Sorry, little man, but this is for big kids only. You head back to the ship and wait for us there," Curtis said.

"Why do you get to go and I can't?"

"I'm the only one of us that knows how to get to the dungeon. You escaped before you had the privilege of experiencing those accommodations."

Edward noted Giuseppe's disappointment and squatted down to look him in the eye. He took the bow off his shoulder and handed it to Giuseppe along with some arrows from his pocket. "Do you know how to use these?"

"Yes, Sir Edward. I've always had great aim."

"Excellent. Well take good care of this. And don't be afraid to use it on your way back in case you encounter any opposition."

Giuseppe nodded. He then looked down at the rope. "Just make sure you hang on. It must be at least two thousand meters from here to the sea."

"And a long way down if we fall," Curtis said. "I worry about my mother. She's not going to like this."

Edward took the remaining rope and placed it on the ground, and he sent the oxen back down the hillside. Then he slipped on the knight's helmet that concealed his face. "How do I look?" he asked.

"Like a knight in shining armor," Giuseppe said with a laugh.

"See you in a bit," Edward said. Then he began running along the forest edge toward the front of the castle.

Edward crouched down amidst the falling rain, which pinged loudly against his helmet, and surveyed the castle entrance. There were guards everywhere, more than he had ever seen in one place. His knight's armor was an asset but not a guarantee of entry, especially now that the castle was on heightened security. Time to get creative.

Creativity had always come naturally to him. As an only child and then an orphan, he had a lot of time by himself to think. His parents, the Duke and Duchess of Highbury, were killed in a barbarian invasion. His uncle, King Harold Wellington, put down the attack and took young Edward in as his own. His early childhood trauma had left him scarred and vulnerable, and he turned to magic as a refuge. He had trouble relating to other people, but he could connect to them through his magic.

By the time he was a teenager, King Harold was realizing his vision of a united Europe. Edward slipped into the shadows, partly because his unique knowledge of the kingdom treasure's location made him a target for the king's enemies, but also because he preferred being on his own. And he loved his uncle and wanted to do his part to help the kingdom. So with his talent for magic and his predilection toward being the lone wolf, espionage was a perfect fit.

He noticed the drawbridge descending over the moat and saw some knights approaching. They took off their masks to show their faces to the guards before proceeding in, and then the drawbridge was raised once more. He was right. It was not going to be possible to just waltz right in like he did yesterday.

Ten minutes had gone by, and he was thinking about his next move, when he saw a horse-drawn wagon coming around the bend toward the castle. There were two men and four horses, and the wagon was covered with a tarp to keep its contents dry. This was an opportunity—it was time to make a play.

The wagon was approaching where he was hiding on the edge of the forest. Once it passed him, he crept from behind and jumped onto the wagon, quietly submerging himself under the tarp without drawing the attention of the coachmen.

The wagon arrived at the gate less than a minute later. Edward had little time to decide if it was worth moving from his spot. He might be seen if he tried to move, but the guards might search under the tarp.

He decided to move. He looked around at the barrels on the wagon and could smell the gunpowder. Invented in the Orient, it had spread to Europe along the Silk Road. Guns had not been invented yet, but that did not stop inventors from trying to find uses for the mysterious and explosive substance.

Around the barrels there was some thin rope. Edward loosened the rope and fed it through the slats of the wagon. While the two coachmen were talking to the guards, he slipped out the back and positioned himself underneath the wagon. The rope he had fed through now hung down far enough for him to grab on to, and he kicked his feet up against the wagon to keep himself hidden.

He had made the right choice, for the guards came around the back and lifted the tarp. Then the wagon proceeded into the castle's courtyard. Once it stopped, the horsemen disembarked and walked indoors, and Edward used the opportunity to slip out from under the wagon. He was walking around the courtyard getting his bearings when he crossed paths with another knight. He thought he might be questioned, and he was relieved when the knight merely nodded and kept walking. Edward nodded back and then continued toward the castle's west side.

He climbed up the stairs to reach the outer wall of the castle, where he and Giuseppe had acted from earlier that morning during the rescue of Prince Curtis. He made his way to the northwest end and waited until the round of guards had passed, and then he waved at Curtis and Giuseppe who were hiding at the edge of the woods.

"Time for me to go," Curtis said when he saw the signal.

"Good luck," Beppe said.

The prince ran quickly up to the moat. Curtis took the end of the large rope and tied it around his shield, and Edward threw another smaller rope which Curtis caught and used to swing his body over the moat and up against the castle wall. He was a good climber and reached the top quickly.

Once at the top, Curtis waved back to Giuseppe, who was still at the edge of the forest where he would be out of sight but able to see what was happening. He saw Edward tie the end of the large rope onto a sconce—the zip line was now up and ready to go.

Curtis looked down at his feet at a fallen knight. "While you were climbing, I found you something to wear," Edward said wryly. Curtis quickly donned the knight's armor, and then they tied up the unconscious knight and locked him behind a nearby door using Edward's key.

They made their way down the stairs, and after a few minutes of navigating through the castle's interior, they reached a long hallway at the end of which were the steps that led down to the musty dungeon. Edward was about to descend when Curtis stopped him.

"Hold on," he said. "We can't just walk down like this. There's a guard at the bottom. He's one of the biggest men I've ever seen. We'll have to think of some way around him—I don't think brute force will do the trick."

Edward paused for a moment to think. "Take off your helmet," he said.

"Why? He'll see me."

"Exactly," Edward said. ♣

The door to the dungeon opened, and the large, burly knight rose from his chair to see two men walking down the steps. It was another knight along with someone who looked like the renegade prince.

"My good man," Edward said, "I have captured this outlaw. Go notify our Queen at once. Tell her to open the cell and throw him in with the others." Edward paused to take the man in. Curtis was right—he was enormous.

"Curtis, oh no!" the Queen of Diamonds exclaimed from inside the cell.

"It's all right, Mother, I'm fine," Curtis said.

"But, what about..." the big man stammered somewhat meekly.

"Go to her, now!" Edward ordered. "I'll stay here with him and guard the others."

"All right," the big man said, and he went up the stairs.

"That was easy!" Curtis said. "I guess his brain isn't the same size as the rest of him."

Edward took out his special key and placed it in the lock of the cell's door. "Let's hope this works," he said.

"Nineteen out of twenty, right?" Curtis said.

The key turned in the lock beautifully and the cell door opened. "Mother! Father!" Curtis exclaimed as he embraced each of them.

"Son, I'm so glad you're all right," the king said. "Who is this that would help us?"

Edward removed his helmet. "It is I, Uncle."

"Edward! My God, what are you doing here?" The king's shock turned to joy at the sight of his nephew whom he had not seen in quite a long time.

"Long story, Uncle, but first we need to get out of here."

"Let's get going then," King Francesco said. Edward put his helmet back on, and the six royals made their way up the stairs.

⚔

Meanwhile, Giuseppe remained outside at the forest's edge looking up at the castle. He was supposed to have gone back to the beach, but his position seemed secure, and he wanted to stay a little longer to see if anything would happen.

He had been watching the castle closely and had noticed guards walking back and forth as before. There had not been any excitement or anything else of note. He wanted to see everyone go down the zip line, but he knew he had to get back to the boat before the others did so that they would not have to wait for him.

He finally decided to turn back toward Daphne and the sea. He had slung the bow over his shoulder and had begun to descend down the hill when he heard a lot of yelling. He quickly turned around and saw the guards on the rampart running down the stairs and then out of view. He could not hear what was being said, but there was a lot of commotion. *What if something is wrong?* he thought to himself. *What if they're in trouble?*

The guards had disappeared, so he had a free run to the castle if he wanted it. He did not know what was best, but his intuition told him to act, so he decided to make a move. He emerged from the forest and ran toward the edge of the moat. The smaller rope that Edward had lowered for Curtis was still there—fortunately no one had seen it. But he would have to cross the moat to get to it.

It was not that far across—only about fifteen meters. He peered down into the water, but it was so murky that he could not see much. He reached his hand in the moat and it felt ice-cold. He was about to jump in when he noticed some movement in the water. He got down on his knees to take a closer look and saw that it was filled with eels swimming wildly about.

"Shoot," he said aloud. He was contemplating what to do when he heard the voices again. He heard one voice in particular that stood out from the rest. "Please, don't hurt anyone else. Enough have suffered already." It was the voice of his father.

That was the only motivation he needed. He jumped into the freezing cold water and swam like a madman. His arms and legs were thrashing about, and he made it to the rope in what took less than ten seconds but felt like a minute. He quickly grabbed the rope and climbed a few feet before pausing and turning to look back down at where he had just been.

The eels had gathered beneath his feet and were looking up at him. Their angry faces seemed to be upset that he had not swum slower. Giuseppe looked down at his body while still holding onto the rope—he did not see or feel any damage. He had miraculously made it across without incident.

He started climbing the rope in earnest and heard the voices getting louder. He got to the top and then ran to the other edge of the rampart to look down into the courtyard. He saw Edward and Curtis, his parents, and Curtis's parents all surrounded by about forty men. Edward still wore a helmet, but Curtis was exposed. And there was the Queen of Spades, standing right in front of them. Giuseppe looked with trepidation on the scene unfolding below. He figured they would need a few more miracles to get out of this one. ♣

ortunately, Giuseppe had the rampart to himself as the guards stationed there had run down to the courtyard. Still dripping wet, he got down on his knees and crept toward the middle of the balcony. He was now in the exact spot where he was almost twenty-four hours ago, when he had used the mirror to help save Prince Curtis. Maybe being in the same place would bring him some good fortune.

He scanned the courtyard to see if anything caught his eye. There, on the opposite side from where he was, were three big barrels about fifteen feet apart. They were in the same area where the barrels were this morning that Edward had blown up. Could it be more gunpowder?

The Jack of Clubs ran over a few feet to a burning torch attached to the wall beneath a slight overhang. He lit the ends of three arrows and ran back to his original spot. He put two of the lit arrows on the ground and was getting the third one ready when he noticed

Curtis looking up at him. Giuseppe pointed to the barrels, and Curtis glanced over and then gave him a nod of understanding.

"Brace yourselves," the Jack of Diamonds said quietly to his fellow captives, "and get ready to run."

Giuseppe raised the arrow and fired. A direct hit! The first barrel exploded with such force that the Queen of Spades and several knights were knocked off their feet. Giuseppe wasted no time in firing the other two arrows.

His aim was true, and the ensuing chaos provided the diversion that Edward needed to lead his group back inside the castle and away from the crowd. Some of the knights gave chase, but Edward locked the door behind them. While the knights scrambled to find a key, the royals got a head start on their way through the castle and back to the zip line near where Giuseppe was.

Giuseppe drew an unlit arrow while surveying the scene. The Queen was slow to get up from the blast, and he had her in his sights. For what seemed like an eternity, he looked at her and contemplated putting an arrow into her body. He thought of what she did to his parents and what she would have done to him. He gripped the end of the arrow with his right hand and wanted more than anything to let it go, but he stopped himself. He did not know why, but it simply did not feel right, and he lowered the bow.

There were knights who had now seen his location, and some of them started running up the stairs after him. He ran along the outer wall and found the nearest door and ducked inside—fortunately, it was unlocked. He found himself on a narrow, second-floor walkway that looked down onto a small dining room, which had a long table and several banners hanging from the ceiling. He immediately ducked down behind the railing, not sure if anyone had seen him enter.

He slowly lifted his head above the railing and was surprised to see that no one else was in the room. On the table were half-eaten plates of food. It looked as if there had been five or six places set for dinner. Perhaps they had been eating and then got up when they heard the explosion.

His eyes scanned the table and then he saw something which startled him: lying face down on the table were the two cards the Queen had stolen! So she had been eating here and then left in a hurry. It was careless of her, Giuseppe thought, to leave the cards lying around—though what would make her think anyone would be around to take them back?

Giuseppe stood up and exhaled. Chaos was reigning outside, and he likely did not have much time to meet the others at the zip line. But the cards were just lying there. He had to get down and get them.

He made his way over to the stairway in the corner and descended down into the dining room. He picked up the two cards and examined them briefly. The Jack of Diamonds and the Jack of Hearts. He had never held nor even seen either of the two red Jacks, and he very briefly lost himself while contemplating where these cards had been and what they represented.

His daze was broken by the noise of a door opening. He immediately turned toward the sound and saw Kiersten enter the room. She had her head down at first, but then she looked up and their eyes met, causing her to startle. Giuseppe felt goose bumps fire through his body. He smiled at her and raised his finger to his mouth in a shushing signal, in the hope that he could implore her to be quiet.

She smiled back at him and nodded her head as if she would do as he asked. But it was a sarcastic gesture, for a second later she screamed with a voice louder than the mightiest trumpet, "MOTHER!"

Giuseppe immediately shoved the cards into his pocket and ran across the room and up the stairs. The door to the outside was in the opposite corner from the stairway. He started running toward the door, but it opened and three knights ran in, blocking his path. Simultaneously, three more knights came in the door that Kiersten had entered from, and they made their way up the stairs toward him from the left. As Kiersten smiled at him from below, he realized he was stuck in the middle.

Trapped. ♣

The knights were running toward him from both directions and would be on top of him in a few seconds. He looked up and saw one of the banners hanging from the ceiling. He climbed onto the top of the railing and jumped into the air. He caught the tapestry with the tips of his fingers, and his momentum enabled him to swing across the other side of the room to the walkway.

He now had a clear path to the door, and he quickly ran outside with the knights close behind in full pursuit. He ran toward the rope and saw a group huddled around the spot where it was tied. Queen Violet and his mother were already cruising down the zip line, and his father was getting ready to go next.

"Dad!" Giuseppe called out. He ran toward his father and gave him a big hug.

"Son, are you all right? We thought you went down to the ship." The king heard noises and looked up to see knights running at them from both directions.

"Dad, I'm sorry. I got us in a lot of trouble here."

"No, no," King Francesco reassured his son even as they were surrounded by at least twenty-five knights. "It's only because of you that we made it this far at all. Everything will be all right."

"I don't think it will," said a voice from the back. Making their way through the crowd was the Queen of Spades and Kiersten, who was grinning with delight. "Nice little stunt you pulled here," the Queen continued. "But the game's over." She turned to look at the man in the knight's outfit that was standing next to the rope.

"You there," the Queen said. "Unmask yourself." The man did as he was told to reveal a familiar face.

"Edward," the Queen said with a hint of amazement and satisfaction. "What a very pleasant surprise! Who needs those filthy cards if I have you? Guards, seize them at once."

Curtis looked over at Edward with a faint hope that Edward had one more trick up his sleeve, but he did not. Their position was hopeless. They were completely surrounded and outnumbered at least five to one. Edward shook his head, and Curtis realized they were doomed.

The knights approached with swords drawn. "What shall we do with them?" one asked. The rain increased to a steady downpour, and the thunder and lightning had returned.

"Tie Edward up. Tightly," the Queen stated. "Kill the rest. All of them. Right here, right now. No more games." ♣

As Curtis prepared to die for the second time that day, he saw from the corner of his eye another man approaching. He was dressed regally, not like one of the knights.

"What's going on here?" the man said in a loud voice.

Everyone turned to see the Jack of Hearts, Prince Enrique, walking toward them. "What's he doing here?" Curtis muttered softly.

"Ah, Prince Enrique, so nice of you to join us. Welcome to our party." Everyone was silent as the Queen spoke. "Where have you been? Obviously you got a case of very cold feet," she said with a condescending laugh.

"Tell them, Enrique," she continued. "Tell them about our plan. How you conspired against them. How you betrayed them."

The kings looked at the prince with questioning glances. "Enrique," the King of Diamonds said, "is it true?"

Enrique looked directly into the King's eyes and walked forward.

"I have no idea what she is talking about."

"Oh you don't, do you?" the Queen raised her voice. "I know where you were, you opportunistic rat. You were waiting to see how this all played out. Waiting to see who got the upper hand. Well, I wasn't going to take you back, not after you left me the way you did."

"The woman is insane," Enrique said. Suddenly he pulled out a small knife, grabbed the Queen, and stood behind her with the blade under her chin.

"Everybody out," he said to the knights. "Get out of here, now! Down the stairs."

The knights did not move.

"I won't ask again," Enrique repeated, pushing the blade so that it was almost piercing the Queen's neck.

"Back off," Schultz said to his men. The knights slowly retreated away from the royals and off the rampart. Kiersten remained, glaring at Enrique with hatred in her eyes.

Enrique turned to Edward. "Go. Get them out of here." Edward turned to his uncle and motioned for him to go. King Harold grabbed a handle and slid down the rope, and he was soon followed by the King of Clubs, Curtis, and Giuseppe. Edward was the last to go. Before leaving, he turned to Enrique who was still holding the Queen. "My good man," Edward said before descending down the line, "one handle left for you. Come join us."

Meanwhile, Kiersten snuck up beside the prince and stabbed him with a knife of her own, a small silver dagger. She thrust it into his upper left thigh, causing him to holler with pain and let go of the Queen. The Queen and Kiersten ran over to the rope and then turned to Enrique, who was lying on the ground. He pulled the knife out of his leg and yelled in agony once again.

"I could have given you everything!" she screamed at him. "Money and power beyond your wildest dreams! Why did you ruin everything?"

"The treasure, yes, I've always wanted it. I've dreamed of it for years. But I didn't need power. Not like you. You killed my parents. Did you think I wouldn't notice that?"

The Queen turned back to the zip line. She thought for a moment about what to do, and when she looked back at Enrique, he was gone. Where did he go?

Suddenly she was pushed from behind. She landed hard on the ground, her fallen crown clattering over the stones. Spinning around, she saw Enrique standing over her. Kiersten let out a maniacal yell and charged him, but he kicked her and she fell. Then he picked up the last handle and went to the zip line.

The Queen lay on the ground and looked up at Enrique, who was about to descend. "We could have had it all," she said.

He turned at the sound of her voice.

"WE COULD HAVE HAD IT ALL!" she yelled at the top of her lungs.

He turned away from her without a word and went down the zip line.

The Queen got to her feet and ran over to the castle's edge. Enraged, she spotted Enrique's crown lying a few yards away. The crown was open at the back, and she placed the half circle over the zip line, grabbed on to each end, and started the descent herself.

"Mother, what are you doing?" Kiersten yelled while running over to the edge. But it was too late. The Queen was already on the way to exact her revenge.

At that moment several of the knights came running back, led by

Schultz. They got to the rope and saw Kiersten standing there with her dagger, still fresh with Prince Enrique's blood.

"What happened? Where's the Queen?" Schultz asked.

Kiersten nodded in the direction of the zip line.

"Everyone, get to the sea," Schultz yelled.

"You're too late for that," Kiersten proclaimed, stopping them in their tracks. She was holding the dagger next to the rope.

"What are you doing, Kiersten?" Schultz asked.

"You won't catch them in time. They're too far ahead. This is the only way."

"You can't cut that rope," Schultz cautioned, slowly raising his sword, though his tone was even sharper.

"It's the only way to get the Jack of Hearts," she said with fire in her eyes. "I have to do it."

"But you'll kill the Queen too. I can't let you do that," Schultz said moving closer.

Kiersten ignored him and abruptly sliced the rope. She picked up her mother's crown from the ground along with the scepter that lay nearby. She placed the crown on her head and looked directly at the big German. "I'm your Queen now," she said.

⚜

The sun had risen in the east, and the rain had ceased, revealing a glorious morn. Everyone was happily reunited on the boat, but they were waiting to see if Enrique would be joining them. Giuseppe was straining his eyes through the lifting fog and suddenly saw him appear.

"Look, there he is!" Giuseppe said, pointing toward the zip line. Then he paused, noticing someone else following closely. "But who's that behind him?" he asked.

Edward stared closely and then recognized the second form. "That's the Queen of Spades," he said while drawing his sword. "She's taking matters into her own hands."

Their anticipation turned to astonishment as they saw the rope falling behind the royals. The Queen did not have a chance. She let out a bloodcurdling scream as she fell two hundred feet to her death into the forest. Enrique, however, instinctively grabbed the rope after hearing her cry. The other end of the rope was still tied to the ship, and he now found himself on a horizontal rope swing. His angular momentum carried him past the ship about one hundred feet, where he landed in the icy waters of the North Sea.

"Enrique!" Curtis yelled. He tossed off his armor and jumped into the frigid ocean. He swam quickly, for Enrique was barely conscious and had started to sink. Once Curtis arrived at the spot where he had seen Enrique go down, he dove into the depths of the sea.

Edward detached a rowboat from the ship and headed their way. He paddled over to the general area where Curtis was last seen. He looked around for any sign of movement and when he saw none, he feared the worst. But after what felt like an interminably long time, Curtis burst above the water with Enrique in his arms only a few meters from the rowboat. Edward helped them in and then rowed them back to the ship. Once aboard, the others quickly dried them off while Queen Giovanna tended to Enrique's leg wound.

"We'd better get out of here before the Queen's army mobilizes," Edward declared. "Trevor!" he yelled to the ship's captain. "Time to set off!"

The small crew manned the sails and the ship began to move. Prince Enrique had awakened but was still dazed. Queen Violet fed him some soup while Daphne huddled around Curtis to help keep him warm. As they sailed toward London, Giuseppe looked back to see the castle on the hill slowly disappear from view. ♣

I t was the dead of night, and it had gotten cold. The fire crackled, and the stars shone brightly in the cloudless sky.

Pierre had finished his lengthy rendition of the legend, and the others were quiet for a few minutes, reflecting on all they had heard.

"What an incredible story," Celine eventually remarked. "I can't believe I've never heard that before. What happened to all of them when they made it back to London?"

"They had a glorious nighttime parade," Pierre said. "A celebration for the ages."

"Sounds amazing!" Celine exclaimed. "What about after that? What became of Curtis and Giuseppe and Kiersten?"

Pierre laughed. "That's a whole other story."

"Well, can we hear it?" Celine asked.

"Sorry, but I'm tired out," Pierre said. "Maybe another time."

"Oh well," Celine said. "It has been one long night. It's probably almost morning already. What did you guys think of all that?" she asked, turning to Jack and Gale.

Jack, seldom at a loss for words, stared into the fire. He took out the dagger he had stolen from the Queen and looked at it while turning it over and over. Was this the same one used to cut the zip line many centuries ago? Was the crown that Celine mockingly wore the same crown that had once sat on the head of the Queen of Spades?

"That couldn't possibly be true," he finally said, looking up at the others. "Could it?"

"I believe it," Pierre said. "I heard the Queen talk about the cards and how one day she'd get what was rightfully hers. You know what else I believe? I believe those cards you had were originals. That's why everyone is after them. That's the only thing that makes sense."

"Well, how did we get them?" Jack asked. "Unless," he paused, "unless we're descendants from royal families. Unless we have royal blood." He turned to Gale. "What do you think?"

Gale shook his head. "I'm no European royal," he said. "I'm an Indian. I don't know how my mother got this card or if it's the real thing, or if it's even a real story."

"Well, some people believe it's real," Celine said. "They were going to kill us back there on the boat."

Jack sighed. "It's a lot to process," he said.

"So now Kingman has all the cards," Celine said. "Do you think he will find the treasure?"

"He won't find it," Pierre said. "Because he doesn't have all the cards."

Jack and Gale both looked up from their downward gazes. "How do you know that?" Jack asked.

Pierre smiled, reached into his pocket, and pulled out the Jack of Spades. "Because the last one's right here," he said proudly. ♣

ack's eyes widened at Pierre's revelation. "Can I see it?" he asked. Pierre got up and handed the card to him. Gale and Celine crowded around Jack and examined the front of the card showing the one-eyed Jack of Spades wearing an unhappy countenance. Then Jack flipped the card over to look at the back. There was a sword in the upper right corner and a shield in the lower left, exactly like the ones they used to possess.

"This looks just like ours! Same color too. How did you get this?" Jack wondered aloud.

"I grabbed it off Erik's body before we left the boat," Pierre said. "I knew he kept it on him. Kingman didn't."

Jack then studied the middle of the card's back. It was a picture of a crooked tree whose trunk had a large, U-shaped bend right in the middle.

"What is this tree?" Jack asked. "Is this where the treasure is hidden?"

"Yes, I think so," Pierre said. "Right beneath that crooked tree."

"So our two cards would tell Kingman what streets to go to," Jack reasoned. "Do you know what was on the back of the Jack of Hearts?"

"A city. The city where the treasure is hidden."

"What city?" Celine asked.

"I don't know," Pierre said. "Neither did the Queen. I don't think anyone knows except Kingman."

"Somewhere where there's a High Street and a Low Street," Gale noted.

"Sounds like England," Jack said. "Or maybe America. So Kingman will go to whatever town is on the back of that card and will find the streets. I guess he figured he knew enough to find the treasure. But once he gets there, he won't know to look under the tree."

"But how big could the intersection of High Street and Low Street be?" Celine observed. "Can't he just dig the whole thing up?"

"If he does, then more power to him," Jack said. "He can have his treasure. I just want to find my brother."

"And I don't care so much for the treasure," Gale said. "I just want my card back. It meant a lot to me."

"Someday," Celine said to Gale, "you'll get your card back. I just know it. And maybe we'll find that treasure too. But first we need to get some sleep. It's been a really long night."

"What are we going to do?" Jack pondered anxiously. "We're being hunted and we don't know where we are. We need to get out of here, and I never did find my brother."

"Your brother—is he named Marco?" Pierre asked.

Jack looked up bewilderedly. "How did you know that?"

"I met him once, only briefly, on the Queen's Caribbean island. She was holding him prisoner. Nice guy. He looks a lot like you."

"He is alive—thank God!" Jack exclaimed. Then he tried to make sense of the new information and put the pieces together.

"She wanted the card," he continued aloud. "Why else would she hold him? But he didn't have it."

"That's right," Pierre said. "He must have been protecting you."

"But how did she get him in the first place, if Kingman was the one who..."

Suddenly it hit him. "They were working together," Jack continued. "He delivered my brother to her. The Coronado Kid."

"And he double-crossed her," Celine interjected. "Just like the Jack of Hearts double-crossed the Queen of Spades those many years ago."

"Your brother's at her American compound," Pierre said. "I've been there. It's in the South, but I don't know where it is from here."

"Well, we're in the South now," Jack said. "Do you remember anything else about where her compound is located?"

Pierre shook his head. "I'm sorry. I just know it's near a town with lots of guards."

Jack played out the scenario in his mind. "She knows now Marco doesn't have the card. And she's not happy about anything that happened today. She'll probably kill him, right?" he asked Pierre.

Pierre hung his head and softly said, "Yes."

Jack put his head in his hands. "I don't know what to do," he said.

Celine put a hand on his back. "Well, the one thing we all need is sleep. Let's get at least a few hours and then we'll figure out our next step."

"I can't sleep right now," Jack responded.

"Let me go and scout our position," Gale proposed. "I'll be back here in an hour or two. Then we can decide in what direction to head."

Jack reluctantly dropped his shoulders. "All right," he said. "We'll wait here."

Gale stood up, grabbed his bow and arrows, and started off into the night hoping to find a clue to tell him where they were, or better yet, where Marco was. ♣

The rhythmic sound of Pierre's snoring was soothing against the cricket's song and the crackling of the fire. Jack lay on his back looking up at the stars, trying to make sense of the long day and wondering what would happen next. He went to reach for his playing card, which he liked to twirl when he was thinking about something. He was saddened to remember that it was gone and that he would probably never see it again.

Celine came over and lay down next to him. She was witty and clever, and Jack enjoyed bantering with her. In the small town where he came from, he knew all the girls and was not really fond of any of them, and it was nice to be on an adventure and meet someone new.

"What's on your mind?" she asked quietly.

"Just a long day," he answered, returning her gaze. Then he looked back up at the stars. "When I left home, I never really expected to find him. Deep down, I thought there was a chance. But it's a big country out there and I'm still a kid. What would I even have done if I had found him?"

"I think it was valiant of you to try," Celine said reassuringly. "You'd do anything for your family—that shows the kind of loyalty and character you have. The King of Clubs would be proud of you."

Jack chuckled. "Do you really believe that whole thing?"

Celine shrugged. "I don't see why not. I've heard more implausible tales in my day, that's for sure."

"What is your story?" he asked. "What are you really doing here?"

Now it was Celine's turn to gaze toward the heavens. "I'm an orphan," she said. "My parents died last year of consumption. I was the only child and the last one left in my family."

"Sorry to hear that," Jack said.

"I still have relatives in New Glarus, but it was time for me to go," Celine continued. "I wanted to get out, see the world, have adventures."

"Well you've accomplished those goals in spades," Jack quipped.

"Clever guy," Celine snickered. "Well, this week certainly went exactly how I planned it. I totally saw myself on the Underground Railroad by a fire in the dead of night with an Indian, an Italian, and an escaped slave, all the while being hunted by the progeny of the real-life Queen of Spades."

"Yeah, if only your adventures were more interesting."

They turned their attention back to the night sky and lay in silence for a few minutes. Jack's eyelids grew heavy and he yawned. "What are you thinking about?" Jack finally asked, breaking the silence.

Celine continued looking skyward. "I'm thinking about all the stories those stars have seen. The kingdoms and civilizations that have risen and fallen. The frailty of life."

"That's all, huh?" Jack said. "Deep thoughts for four in the morning, or whatever it is."

"When I think back to olden times," Celine continued, "I can't help but be humbled by the miracle of our existence."

"What do you mean?" Jack asked.

"Well let's just say you *are* related to those Clubs from the story. If they had died that night in Queen Ingrid's castle, you wouldn't be here. Multiply and compound that destiny, luck, or whatever you want to call it by hundreds of generations. What if my parents had never met? Or what if my fiftieth great-grandparents had never met? Either way, it's the same thing—I wouldn't be here today."

"I guess I'd never thought of it like that before," Jack said before succumbing to an enormous yawn. "Everyone's life is kind of like a miracle when you put it that way."

"Yeah," Celine said. "It's a wonder we don't treat each other better knowing that."

"Well it was nice talking philosophy with you, but I can barely keep my eyes open."

"Yeah, I guess we won't solve the world's problems tonight, but it was nice talking to you, Mr. Jack of Clubs."

"Yeah, that's me. Just your regular Italian nobleman."

"I think it's time to finally get some sleep," Celine said.

"Sounds good," Jack replied sleepily.

Celine snuggled closer to him and put her head on his chest. Jack wrapped his right arm around her and they quickly drifted off to sleep. ♣

The sun shone briefly through the increasingly cloudy sky, but it quickly retreated and a light rain started to fall. Gale had been running for about two miles through the forest parallel to a dusty, narrow road. He figured the road would lead somewhere, but he preferred to stay in the shadows to avoid being spotted.

He had only found the road due to his tracking ability. Earlier, in the depths of the forest, he had noticed some disturbed dirt and a broken branch, which signified that someone had passed through recently. He followed some additional signs, hidden to the average person, until he reached the road. As a boy, he frequently explored the woods with his father, and it was there that Gale learned the language of nature while developing a keen eye and cultivating instincts.

He continued on, not sure where he was going, but hoping to find a landmark that would give him some idea where they were and how they should proceed. He did not want to venture too far, and he was getting ready to turn back, when he came upon a clearing and saw a bridge up ahead. He cautiously crept out into the open and walked toward it.

The bridge spanned a small river that was at least seventy feet below. There was no clearing on the other side—only the road surrounded by more woods. Gale quickly crossed the bridge and got back into the trees and continued onward.

A few minutes later he approached another clearing which opened up onto a hill. He continued to the top of the crest and looked down. He was surprised to see a one-street town where people were milling about despite the light rain.

On the other side of the valley, there was a large structure that overlooked the town and was unlike anything Gale had ever seen. It was completely black, and there were turrets on all sides.

Was this the Queen's American compound that Pierre spoke of? *It probably was*, Gale thought. *Who else would have a European-style castle in the middle of the Southern countryside?*

Gale continued to scan the surroundings from his perch atop the hill, and his attention was caught by a steel cage right in the middle of the street. There was a man inside, and a few passersby mocked him as they strolled past. When the man turned around, Gale could see his face, and despite the distance, Gale was pretty sure it was Jack's brother.

Gale went behind the hill and lay on his back while pondering his next move. He looked up at the sky and was lost momentarily in the slow, peaceful clouds. The sprinkling rain on his face felt good and reminded him of the Great Spirit working through Mother Nature. Even though he was dead tired, and he had little hope of freeing Jack's brother by himself, he felt the Spirit telling him to press onward.

He got up and walked down the other side of the hill without a plan in place. He was just going to wing it. ♣

ightingale walked down the street and passed a few people who looked at him quizzically. He stood out in this white Southern town and he knew it. The cage with the prisoner was about fifty yards away. Gale continued to move toward him, still not at all sure what he would do once he got there.

Then, on the left side of the street, he saw an old Indian standing over a large pot of soup. Gale had an idea and walked closer to the old man. "Good morning," he said as he approached.

The man had a wrinkled face which brightened up at the sight of the boy. He had dark skin and long black hair, and his clothes looked as old as he was. He nodded and replied in an Indian language that Gale did not understand.

Gale pointed at the soup and held up one finger as a request for a bowl of soup. Gale removed the bow from around his shoulder and extended it. "I don't have money," he said, "but you can have this."

The old man ignored the bow and dished out a large bowl of bean and rice soup. It was very hot and smelled delicious. The man handed the soup to Gale, and when Gale re-offered the bow, the man shook his head no. "A gift from the Great Spirit," the man said in broken English.

"Thank you," Gale said, and he bowed his head toward the old Indian before walking away with the bowl of soup in hand.

As he moved closer to the cage, he got a better look at the person inside and was now certain it was Jack's brother. When he was within ten yards, a man sitting outside the nearby saloon got up to meet him. He was a big man and was wearing two guns.

"Whatchya doin' young 'un?" the man asked.

"The old Indian down the street wants to give the prisoner a bit of food," Gale replied.

"Well, you a little injun too, ain't ya?" the man replied. "Ah go ahead. He be dead tonight anyway." The man smiled at the prisoner and then spat on the ground on his way back to where he was sitting.

Gale walked up to the cage and offered the soup through the bars.

"Thank you," the prisoner said, taking the soup. "I'm starving." He quickly drank some of the hot liquid and then reached in and scooped up a handful of beans.

"Are you Marco?" Gale said softly.

The prisoner stopped eating and moved closer to Gale. He looked around and then whispered back, "Yeah. How'd you know that?"

"My name is Gale. Your brother Jack is near. He's my friend. Right now we're on the run."

Marco's eyes widened. "Jack? What's he doing here? How did he find me?"

"It's a long story," Gale replied. "I don't have much time. Anything you can tell me will be helpful, like where we are and what's going to happen to you."

Marco leaned in and lowered his voice. "Mine is also a long story," he whispered, "but the short version is there's a crazy woman who calls herself the Queen and owns that castle up there." Marco pointed at the large fortress looming over them.

"Yeah, we've met, unfortunately," Gale said.

"Really?" Marco said. "So you know all about her then. Well, she's going to kill me tonight at eleven o'clock. All over some stupid playing card that she wanted. Which I don't even have—Jack has it, but I don't know how she found about it or why she wants it. Anyway, she's done with me and is going to hang me tonight in the castle courtyard."

"Why does she have you out in the street like this?"

"To humiliate me."

"Well, Jack wants to rescue you," Gale said. "How many men does she have here?"

"A lot," Marco said. "Probably at least thirty out-of-work Confederate guns for hire. Tell Jack to stay away from here. I don't want to see him get caught up in this. Plus it's more important that you and he spread the word about her plot—there's much more at stake than just me."

"What is that?" Gale asked.

Marco looked over his shoulder and leaned in even closer. "She's hired a man named Booth to kill President Lincoln. Tonight in Washington. She and Booth confessed it to me while I was imprisoned on her island in the Caribbean. She told me for her own amusement, knowing that she was going to kill me anyway."

"Why would she kill the President?" Gale asked.

"She has friends at all levels of the Union and Confederate governments. Lincoln has many enemies. This act will convince them of her power, causing them to come out and support her as the ruling monarch of the United States. That's the first goal of her master plan. Then it's the Caribbean, and eventually control over the entire Western Hemisphere."

"And the diamond treasure," Gale said while trying to piece things together, "will finance her operation."

"Indeed it will, for I will get my hands on it very soon," a nearby voice said.

They were both so wrapped up in their conversation that they did not notice someone approaching from behind until it was too late. Gale turned around to see the Queen standing right there, looking down on him with contempt. ♣

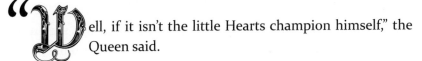

"Well, if it isn't the little Hearts champion himself," the Queen said.

About ten of her men came out of the shadows and stood in the street off to the side just watching.

"How did you find us?" the Queen asked. "And where are your wretched friends?"

"Why don't you let him go?" Gale said. "We don't have the cards any more. He's of no use to you. We'll get out of here and won't bother you again."

"See, you're wrong about that," the Queen replied. "One of you still has my Jack of Spades. And did you really think I'd forget about this?" She rolled up her sleeves to show large burn marks from the incident on the boat. "Or about what you did to my son?" she said with a rising voice.

"We told you," Gale said. "Kingman did that."

"This one dies tonight," the Queen uttered while pointing to Marco. Then she looked at Gale. "I think I'll keep you around and kill you too. And if your friends want to come and watch, they're welcome to."

Gale quickly reached into the cell and grabbed Marco's cup of soup. There was still a little soup left inside the cup, and Gale threw the warm, frothy mixture into the Queen's face.

As the Queen shrieked in pain, Gale ran at lightning speed toward the left side of the street. He ducked in an alley between a bank and a hotel and then made his way up the hill. Bullets started flying around as the Queen's men shot at him and gave chase. One of them yelled out, "We'll get the little runt! We'll tar him and burn him alive!" Gale could hear the men yelling with anticipation, and that motivated him even more to pick up the pace.

Though he was much younger than his pursuers, he was incredibly fast over distance, and he began to gain ground. Eventually he got to the top of the hill and made it to the forest. He looked over his shoulder and saw the Queen's men out of firing range, but that did not stop some of them from firing their pistols. He also noticed a few men on horseback heading toward him. There was no way he could outrun the horses, but maybe he could lose them in the trees.

After some hard running through the brush of the forest, he finally made it to the river. But the bridge was nowhere in sight—he must have wandered farther upriver. He paused a moment to think. He could jump in, but it was pretty far down and there did not seem to be an easy way back up.

His thinking was interrupted by the sound of voices. He turned around and saw a few men on their way toward him through the trees. He looked up and saw a long vine hanging down from the tree next to him. Instinctively he grabbed the vine and ran a few steps backward. Then just as the gunmen were upon him, he ran forward at full speed and swung across the ravine. He barely made it to the other side, and he immediately let go and started running through the clearing toward the woods. Some shots rang out, but he was quickly out of range.

He disappeared into the forest and started moving south until he found the road he had come in on. Just as before, he stayed near the road but far enough into the forest that he would not be spotted. Occasionally, a few horsemen rode by, and he would drop to the ground to avoid detection.

Eventually he reached the point where he had come upon the road, and it did not take him much longer to track his way back to the camp. He was completely exhausted and his lungs burned, but the adrenaline of the escape and the news that he had learned had kept him going.

He ran into the camp and saw everyone still there. "Listen up," he gasped. "You'll never believe what I..." He stopped suddenly when he noticed a woman sitting there holding a gun. Immediately he reached for his bow and drew an arrow, but before he could raise his arms, he collapsed out of exhaustion. ♣

It was clear and cool, the perfect day for a hunt. Nightingale woke at sunrise and embarked on a search for deer. He stopped by a stream and caught a few fish for breakfast and then disappeared into the woods. At one point he came face to face with a brilliant stag. He had intended to kill it, but the stag was so accepting of him, so trusting, that Gale was moved to let him go.

After a long but fulfilling day of hunting, exploring, and communing with nature, Gale slept under the stars. As he did every night before shutting his eyes, he took out his Jack of Diamonds and touched its face while giving thanks for all he had in this world. The next morning he made the long journey back to his home, an adobe hut in the desert where he lived with his parents. It was an isolated spot, for there were no other inhabitants living within miles.

He liked being by himself, though sometimes he wished he had some friends around. There were several towns closer to the edge of the desert, including a school that he attended with other Indian children from a different tribe. He ran seven miles each way to reach the school, giving him high levels of fitness and endurance.

As he approached the hut, it was very quiet, and he had the uncomfortable sensation that something was wrong. He ran to the hut and entered through the doorway and saw that his home had been ransacked. All of their possessions were displaced or broken, and there were shattered pots all over the floor. It almost appeared like someone was looking for something.

Who would do this? His family had always gotten along well with their Indian and white neighbors. And where were his parents? He called out to them but heard no response.

He went outside the hut and around to the back where his father grew maize and berries. The storm cloud that had formed overhead finally opened up and dumped a heavy rain onto the dusty desert. The visibility had decreased, and Gale strained to see in any direction. Then he walked around to the other side of the crops. It was there that he saw his parents' lifeless bodies lying on the ground.

He ran over to them and got down on his knees to hold their hands. He had been taught at a young age that real men did not show their emotions, that they never cried. But he could not help himself. The sight of his dead mother and father stirred in him a feeling of sadness and helplessness that he had never felt before. As of that moment, he was completely and totally alone.

♙

He awoke with a start. Sometimes he would have the nightmare and it would feel so real again. He looked around and saw Jack, Celine, Pierre, and the mystery woman standing over him.

"How long have I been out?" he said drowsily.

"About half an hour," the distinguished woman said with a deep voice.

"Who are you?" Gale asked.

Pierre smiled proudly. "This is Moses herself, Harriet Tubman," he said.

"Remember the Underground Railroad we were talking about?" Jack chimed in. "She's the greatest conductor who ever lived—a legend."

"What's she doing here?" Gale wondered.

"I've come to get Pierre and take him back to his mother in Canada," Harriet said.

"How did you find us?" Gale asked.

"Boy, I could find a flea on a dog's back faster than you drew that bow at me. Fact is, I've been looking for this boy for some time. I promised his mother I'd find him. And I finally did. I know a lot of people, and people talk. And I listen."

"We were waiting for you," Jack said to Gale. "And now we're gonna get moving. We'll all head up North and get out of this danger zone."

"Don't you want to know what I found?" Gale asked.

"You found something?"

"Your brother. I talked to him."

Jack was stunned. "Marco? You saw him?"

"Yes," Gale responded. He proceeded to tell them the entire story, including his brush with the Queen and his harrowing escape.

"I'm going to try to save him. I don't care what he told you," Jack said.

"There's one more thing," Gale added. "He told me that the Queen is having someone kill the president tonight in Washington."

Celine gasped, and Harriet shook her head. "We can't let that happen," Harriet declared. "He's a good man. A great man."

"What are we going to do?" Celine lamented. "There are many things to do and not enough time to do them in."

Jack paused for a moment in thought. "The way I see it," he finally said, "we have three objectives that we'll have to divide and conquer. First, Harriet needs to get Pierre out of here safely so he can reunite with his mother."

"Amen," Harriet said.

"Next," Jack continued, "I need to rescue my brother tonight."

"I'm staying with you," Celine said.

"Well," Jack said to Gale, "that means all you have to do is save the President of the United States."

Gale shook his head. "Sure, no problem," he said sarcastically. "It's ironic that it takes an Indian to save the U.S. government after all it has done to us."

"Indeed it is, Mr. Gale," Harriet said. "Now there's a train station in Desortesville a few miles north of here. I'll take you there, and then you can catch the train to Lexington which continues in a direct line to Washington. With luck, you can make it by nightfall."

"What will I do once I'm there? I don't think anyone will believe me if I say that the Queen of Spades wants to kill the president."

"You may not be successful. In fact, you probably won't be," Harriet said. "But all you can do is try."

Gale proceeded to gather his things together in preparation for leaving with Harriet and Pierre, and he gave Jack detailed directions on how to get to the castle.

"Take this," Gale said, offering up his bow and arrows. "You'll need it more than I."

"Thanks," Jack said. "Good luck to you tonight."

"Yes, good luck to you too. I hope you get your brother back."

Jack and Celine both gave him a hug. "Where are you going afterwards?" Jack asked.

"No idea," Gale replied.

"Well, you're always welcome to come live with us in Neffs."

"Thanks Jack."

And with that, Gale and Pierre followed the fearless Tubman as she plowed ahead through the forest. Soon they got to Desortesville, and Harriet pointed Gale in the direction of the train station while also giving him some money for his travels. As they exchanged farewells, Pierre pulled the Jack of Spades from his pocket and handed it to Gale.

"Here," Pierre said. "I'd like you to have this."

"Thank you," Gale said. "But why me?"

"Because I want you to find that treasure someday."

Gale took the card and made his way to the station where he boarded the train to Lexington. Conveniently, he did not have to change trains—the same one would take him all the way to D.C. Once aboard the comfortable train, he fell asleep instantly and barely stirred until the train arrived in Washington. ♣

A light rain continued to fall, and there was a chill in the evening air. Celine had been tucked under a bed of leaves and got several hours of much needed rest. When she awoke after her long nap, she saw Jack sitting on a log, deep in thought and holding the bow that Gale had given him.

"Hey Jack, what time is it?" she called out.

"Almost seven o'clock."

"Seven o'clock? Wow, I slept for a long time. Did you get some sleep?"

"Yeah, I got a little," Jack said, "but it's hard to sleep knowing my brother is about to be executed."

Celine got up, sat on the log next to him and held his hand. "I'm sorry," she said looking into his eyes. "This whole thing is just terrible."

Jack nodded. "Yeah, I know." He paused for a moment before continuing. "Look, I know you want to help, and I appreciate it, but I don't want anything bad to happen to you. It's too dangerous."

Celine leaned forward and gave him a gentle kiss. "I'm coming with you," she said. "Now what's the plan?"

Jack momentarily lost his train of thought after their kiss. He quickly forced himself to refocus, saying, "Better to wait until dark, when they can't see us coming."

"You sound just like Prince Edward."

"I hopefully I can shoot arrows like Prince Giuseppe."

"So once we get there, what do we do?"

"Honestly, I don't know. I think we're better off making it up as we go along. But we should probably get moving soon, since we don't know exactly where we're going, other than from Gale's directions. And this is one time when showing up late to the party is not an option."

He took some nearby mud in his fingers and started spreading it on his cheeks. Celine started to laugh, but he was not in a laughing mood. "What are you doing?" she asked.

"War paint, like Prince Curtis used," he answered.

"Here, let me have some of that too," she said as she began applying the mud to herself. She also put the Queen's crown on. "As long as I'm going to a castle, I might as well dress the part," she added.

They cleaned up their camp and then followed Gale's instructions for getting to the road. Like Gale, they stayed in sight of the road but remained in the forest. They had only a few miles to go before reaching their destination, where danger awaited. ♣

The sun set in the west, and the castle was now shrouded in darkness. They had made it over the bridge while it was still light and had then treaded carefully through the town. They went up the hill undetected and now had a full view of the castle. There was a nearby grove of oak trees that provided some cover while they planned their next move.

Luckily for them there was no moat to deal with, but there were several guards around the perimeter. On the left outer wall there was a set of steps that went up to the castle rampart. The only tricky part would be eluding the two guards in front.

"It's time," Jack said, and he took out his matches and lit one of his arrows. He fired it so that it landed about fifty yards away from the guards. As he had hoped, the guards immediately ran toward the flaming arrow, allowing him and Celine to make a quick dash toward the castle wall and up the stairs.

They got to the top balcony and looked down into the courtyard.

"Whoa," Celine said. "This looks just like the way I pictured the castle in the story, complete with the falling rain."

To Jack's delight, there were large barrels around the courtyard with what he presumed was gunpowder.

"I guess they didn't learn their lesson after six hundred years," he said while pointing to the barrels.

"What if they don't contain what you think they do?" Celine asked.

"Let's just hope they do," he replied. He checked his watch and it read ten minutes before eleven.

⚕

The Queen was inside at her telegraph station checking for updates from her people in Washington. But it was time to put that aside and focus on the matter at hand.

"Schmidt," she called out. "Bring out the prisoner. Time for a show."

Suddenly Jack and Celine saw Marco being led out into the courtyard with his hands and feet tied. Jack felt a surge of adrenaline rush through him. The next few minutes were the most critical of his life. But in order to do his job, he needed to be calm and focused. He closed his eyes briefly and took three large, deep breaths.

Jack took out the Queen's dagger and gave it to Celine. "I'm going to aim for the gunpowder," he said. "I'll also put one through Marco's rope. When I do that, you run down and cut his hands and feet. Hopefully the barrels will explode and provide cover for you. Then run back up with him and we'll get out of here."

"You can hit that rope?" Celine asked surprisingly.

"I have to," Jack said.

"All right, I'm ready," she said as she moved into position near the stairs on the inside part of the rampart.

Even in the rain, there was a drummer who played as Marco was marched to the noose, and a hangman was there to perform the task. As Marco's head was slipped inside the rope, Jack drew his bow.

The platform dropped, and Marco started to hang. Jack fired an arrow but missed on the first try. *Come on! You may not get another chance!* He focused harder than he ever had and let the second arrow fly.

It was a direct hit. The arrow slit the rope apart and Marco fell to the ground. Jack quickly sprang into action by lighting some more arrows and firing them at the barrels. They contained a large amount of gunpowder, and the explosions were massive. Several of the men near the barrels were leveled, and there was confusion in the courtyard.

Celine ran down the stairs and made a direct line for Marco. She reached him and freed his hands and legs with the dagger. Meanwhile, the Queen lay on the ground, bowled over by an explosion, and Jack had her in his sights. He could end it right now, as Giuseppe could have many years ago. As his hand gripped the arrow, time slowed down. He wanted to let go. He told himself to let go. But something inside him stopped him at the last second. He did not know what it was, but he lowered the bow.

Celine and Marco ran toward the stairs, but by this time several of the men had come to their senses and started shooting. Marco made it up the stairs and saw Jack waiting for him.

"Jack, that was great!" Marco exclaimed. "Let's get out of here!" But Jack was looking down at the courtyard in dismay.

While they were running, Celine had slipped and fell in the mud. Schmidt picked her up and put a gun to her head. "Come down right now, or this is the last you see of your girlfriend," he yelled.

Marco turned to Jack. "I know you don't want to hear this, but we should leave. If we go back down there, we all die."

Jack shook his head. "I may as well be dead if I don't go down there, I wouldn't be able to live with myself."

"Well, then I'm going with you," Marco said, and they walked down the steps with their hands up.

The Queen walked over to them and smiled. "I thought you might show up," she said proudly. "You almost got away with it too. Only this time, I'm going to finish the job. If my ancestor had been as decisive, my family would have assumed power long ago. But better late than never! Let's just keep it simple: guns and bullets."

She walked over to Celine who was still wearing the crown. Celine took it off and tossed it about ten yards away. The Queen simply smiled, walked over to the crown, and put it back on her head.

She turned to Schmidt. "Line them up against the wall over there." Schmidt did as he was told, and the three stood with their backs against the wall, facing the Queen.

"Time for the firing squad," she announced. She called all her men over and formed them in a straight line across from Jack, Celine, and Marco.

"On my count," she yelled. "Ready... Aim..." ♣

The train came to a stop and Gale woke up slowly. He had a great rest and was feeling refreshed. He looked out the window at the big train yard and heard a loud voice call out, "Final stop: New Jersey Avenue Station!"

He got out of the car and walked into the station. It was bustling with people going about their Friday night plans. Gale was out of his element in this large city. *What am I doing here? How can I possibly stop a presidential assassination? I don't know a single person in town or even where I am going.*

He looked at the large clock in the station. The hands read ten after eight. Since he did not know what to do, he decided to simply begin walking. He had heard of the White House—maybe he could start there.

As he headed out of the station, he passed a newspaper cart tended to by a young boy about his age selling papers. "Extra! Extra! Read all about it! War over! President Lincoln at the theatre tonight to celebrate!"

Gale's ears perked up and he walked over to the boy and bought a paper. Fortunately his reading skills were good, the result of many lessons from Miss Jones, the auburn-haired instructor from his Indian school.

He scoured the newspaper for details. An article on the first page read, "President Lincoln, Mary Todd, General Grant, and Julia Grant will be on hand this evening at Ford's Theatre to take in the uproariously entertaining play, *Our American Cousin*. Starting at 7:45, the play is sure to be a hit with the First Family and their companions, the victorious General and his wife. The entertainment will surely be a welcome relief from the long stress of war, and it signifies a return to normalcy for the nation."

Gale looked back at the clock. The play had already started. He turned back to the newspaper boy. "Excuse me," he asked. "Can you tell me how to get to Ford's Theatre?"

"Sure," the boy said. "Just go two blocks north to E street and then about a mile west until you get to Tenth Street."

The sun had set and it was almost completely dark, but there was still a small glimmer of light on the horizon. Gale now knew in which direction to head. "Thank you," he said, and he started to run as fast as he could.

☟

He got to Tenth Street in a short time. There were many people out enjoying the evening on the bustling streets. At first he was not sure where to go, but when he looked up to the north he saw a huge crowd of people lingering. He thought that would be a good place to start and made his way over to join the onlookers.

Suddenly a carriage pulled up and the crowd began buzzing. President Lincoln emerged and a great cheer went up among the people.

He waved to the crowd and then helped his wife step down, after which two more people descended from the carriage.

"That's not General Grant with the president," an onlooker said.

Gale was struck by the president's size. He was extremely tall, and his large hat and shorter wife made him look even taller. The president had a smile on his face and seemed genuinely happy to be there, despite being late to the show. He waved once more to the crowd and then entered the theatre.

After the president was gone from view, Gale fought his way through the crowd and looked at the theatre up close. There were several doors, but only one was being used as the entrance, and there were two theatre employees collecting tickets in front of it. There was another man standing in front of the other doors to keep people out.

Gale did not know what to do. Should he tell those men that the president was being targeted? He was standing there for about a minute, watching the entrance and trying to decide what to do, when a man came from behind and stood next to him. The man was of average height and build and had dark hair and a mustache. He was dressed completely in black, from his boots and pants to his coat and hat, and he had a dashing, debonair quality.

"Are you thinking what I'm thinking?" he said to Gale in a mild Southern accent.

"I don't know, what are you thinking?" Gale replied.

"I'm thinking I want to see the play, but I have no ticket," the man said.

"Yes, I'm in the same predicament," Gale said.

"What's your name?" the man asked.

"Gale. What's yours?"

"Booth, but you can call me J.W.," the man responded.

Gale tried not to display any outward sign that he immediately recognized the name as the one Marco had mentioned, but he must have shown something because Booth's expression became more serious.

"What is it?" he asked. "Do you know me?"

"Ah, no sir. I don't believe I do."

"Well then, Mr. Gale, I venture to say that someday you, along with the rest of the world, will know my name," he said with a chuckle. "But not yet. There is still work to be done."

"What kind of work?" Gale asked.

"Oh, nothing really," Booth said coolly. "Just simple things like the rise and fall of nations and governments. Fortune and fate. What do you say, Mr. Gale, about getting into this theatre and watching that play?"

"Yes sir, I'd like that," Gale said.

"Then come with me," Booth said. He walked toward the entrance and Gale followed closely behind. When he got to the two men collecting tickets, he pulled out a card from his pocket to show them.

"Ah, Mr. Booth," one of the men said. "You don't need to show us your actor's card. We know who you are. Come right in!"

"Excellent! Thank you good sirs," Booth said. "And would you mind if I brought my little friend in? He's studying to be an actor."

"Absolutely," the other man said. "Enjoy the show!"

"We certainly will!" Booth replied.

Gale felt a sense of panic. He wished he had more time to analyze the situation and determine what move was best. It was like a card game, only with less defined rules and much higher stakes. At cards, he could always keep his emotions in check and stay relaxed. This was different.

Should he say something to the ticket collectors? If so, he had to act in the next few seconds.

No, he thought. They would not believe him, and Booth would no longer invite him in. He had to stay close to Booth and buy some time.

Booth opened the theatre doors, and they were met by the sounds of laughter and applause. ♣

hey made their way up to the second floor balcony. There was not a seat to be had, so they sat down on the steps in the back near the last row. The audience was enjoying the play, as evidenced by the constant laughter, and the president seemed to be having a good time as well. From their vantage point, they could clearly see him on their right, sitting in a special box overlooking the stage. There were several flags hanging out of the box, along with a portrait of George Washington on the outside of the box's overlook.

Gale's mind raced as he sat next to Booth, who was laughing uproariously along with the crowd. There was a nearby doorway that led to a small hallway, which in turn led to a second doorway that opened directly into the president's box. Outside the first doorway, a guard sat in a chair watching the play.

What was Booth's plan? Would he overwhelm the doorman by force? Was the doorman in on the plan? Gale did not know what to do, but he thought that as long as he stayed near Booth, he could react when the assassin finally made his move.

⚔

About an hour and a half had passed and nothing had changed. Gale still sat next to Booth on the step, and the Lincolns remained in the box. Gale was starting to wonder if maybe Marco got the name wrong or if there was even a plan at all.

Then suddenly Booth got up without a word and went over toward the doorman. Gale felt his pulse rise quickly—it could be happening now!

Booth said a few words to the doorman, and the doorman opened the door for Booth. After Booth disappeared, Gale sprang up and ran over to the doorman and whispered loudly, "He's going to kill the president! Open the door!"

"What?" the man sneered. "Who are you? Keep your voice down! You'll disturb the audience."

Gale reached around him and tried to open the door but it was locked. Booth must have secured it from behind after he went in.

"What are you doing? Stop that!" the doorman sneered.

Gale turned around and looked down at the stage. He realized he had about ten seconds to think of something. He could not see the president from his current angle, but he could see the American flag hanging down from the edge of the president's box.

Suddenly the audience laughed harder and louder than they had all evening.

In a flash, Gale climbed onto the edge of the balcony and grabbed the fabric of the flag. He jumped off the balcony and swung himself upward. At the height of his ascent, he let go and landed on his feet in the box. He was face to face with Abraham Lincoln. ♣

t the moment that Gale landed on his feet, the door behind the president opened and Booth was standing there. Minutes ago he seemed happy and was laughing at the play. Now he looked deranged and evil as he brandished a small derringer.

"Mr. President!" Gale screamed, and he jumped on Lincoln and pushed him down to the ground. A shot rang out, but the sudden movement had caused Booth to miss the target. Booth quickly pulled out a knife, but Henry Rathbone, the other man in the theatre box, sprung up and landed a right hook on Booth's face.

By this time the crowd had heard the commotion and the play had stopped. The audience members were all standing and trying to see what was happening. They saw Lincoln get up quickly and grab Booth, who was still disoriented from the punch. Lincoln pushed Booth toward the railing, and then he delivered a perfect right uppercut that sent Booth flying off the balcony and onto the stage.

The audience applauded and roared with delight. It was the loud-est they had been all evening—even the actors were applauding. As Booth lay unconscious on the stage floor, officers rushed up the stairs and got to work breaking down the box door.

Meanwhile, Lincoln turned to Gale.

"Young man," he said in his distinctive prairie twang, "I must say, this play was lasting so long that I had wished I was dead. My wish was almost granted."

Gale could not help but smile at the president's gallows humor.

Lincoln smiled back. "Thank you, young man, for what you did tonight," he said earnestly.

Within the next few moments, the officers broke through the door and surrounded the president as a precautionary measure.

"Take this boy back to the White House where he'll be safe," Lincoln said to one of the men. "Find out everything he knows and then report back to me." Then he turned to Gale and said, "I'll have some work to do tonight as a result of this, but why don't you get a good night's sleep and then we'll talk again in the morning."

Gale was ushered out of the theatre and into a carriage, and as they rode away, Gale told the officer all about Marco, Jack, and the Queen. Within minutes, Gale was being led into a place he never thought he would visit—the White House. ♣

ale woke up gradually from a restful night of sleep. The sun trickled through the curtains and a slight breeze blew in through the partially open window. It was the most comfortable bed that Gale had ever slept in, and he had not woken up at all during the night despite having rested most of the day on the train.

He slowly came to his senses and looked around the guest room. There were many paintings, mostly of people he did not know, but he did recognize Thomas Jefferson. Over the bed he noticed an oil canvas of several Iroquois playing lacrosse.

He got out of bed and walked over to the clock. It was tall and looked very old. It read eight-thirty—he had really slept! He got dressed and then opened his bedroom door, not sure where he would be or what he would find. There was an older man sitting in a chair in the hallway, and he smiled when he saw Gale.

"Ah, Mr. Gale, I hope you had a good night's rest. I'm Maxwell, the White House butler. The president asked me to bring you to his office after you were up and had something to eat. First we can go downstairs to the kitchen where Mae will fix you up some breakfast."

Gale walked with Maxwell through the quiet hallways and down a set of stairs. They eventually arrived at the kitchen where they were greeted warmly by Mae, a heavyset woman with a cheery disposition.

"Good mornin' Mr. Gale! What can I get for ya' today?" Mae asked.

"Steak and eggs would be wonderful, if you have that," Gale replied.

"If I have that?" Mae exclaimed, pretending to be insulted. "My boy, Aunt Mae's got everything you could ever dream up. Just say the word and ya' shall receive!"

Gale devoured the steak and eggs so quickly that Mae made him a second helping, and he also put the finishing touches on some delicious biscuits and gravy. When he was done, Maxwell returned and said that the president was ready to see him. Gale followed the butler up some stairs and through some more rooms until they arrived at the Oval Office.

Gale walked into the hallowed room and saw President Lincoln sitting behind his desk reading some telegrams. The president immediately rose to his feet to welcome the boy.

"Young man," the president said while extending a hand, "words cannot express the gratitude that I feel for what you have done. You risked your life to save mine and showed uncommon valor and quick thinking in the face of danger."

"Thank you, sir," Gale said.

"I read the transcript of your account, and I want you to know that we sent federal officers to the castle that you described. Those officers successfully rescued your friends Jack, Celine, and Marco."

Gale felt a surge of excitement and relief. "That's great news. Thank you sir."

"They arrived not a moment too soon," the president continued, "for it was at that time that your friends who had been captured were about to be executed."

Gale shook his head. *What a close call.*

"We also captured many dangerous outlaws at the castle thanks to your information," the president added, "although Queen Brunhilde slipped away in the crossfire. The officers think she got out through a trap door or secret room. But we will keep looking for her, and it's only a matter of time before we get her. In fact, this morning we sent a U.S. naval ship to her Caribbean island and freed the slaves that were living there."

President Lincoln leaned on his desk and folded his hands. "We also retrieved your winnings and Jack's too. We have paid Jack already, and I will see to it that you get the money you're entitled to before you leave here today. Which brings me to a question. Where will you go? Do you have a place to go?"

Gale hesitated a moment. "I'd like to go to Neffs, Pennsylvania," he finally said.

"All right," the president said. "We can get a carriage to take you there."

As Gale glanced around the room at the various artifacts in the famous office, the president walked over to a tall cabinet and opened the right-most door. He pulled something from the bottom and brought it over to Gale.

"I received this from Queen Victoria when she came to the States last year. I'd like you to have it as a gift from me. It's pretty heavy, just so you're aware," the president said with a smile as he handed it to Gale.

Gale took the gift and realized that the president spoke the truth—it was heavy. The back was golden, and even while holding it, he was not quite sure what it was until he turned it over.

It was a large, beautiful shield with the left half painted blue and the right half painted red. It looked to Gale much like Pierre's description of the shield that Prince Curtis had carried long ago. In the middle, there was a dragon being slayed, and its attacker was nothing but a small bird: the Nightingale. ♣

It was Sunday morning and the church was rocking with song. The coastal Canadian town had a diverse population including Norwegians, French Acadians, and escaped slaves from the West Indies. Everyone was welcome at the church service where the music was spirituals in the African tradition.

It was an old, small church with about twenty pews and an aisle down the middle. On this day it was a full house, and the congregation had just finished a somber rendition of "Nobody Knows the Trouble I've Seen." The preacher, a middle-aged man born in Cameroon, had started to discuss the reading of the day when the big door in the back opened and a woman walked in.

The preacher noticed the woman and continued to preach, but he paused after she kept walking to the front of the church. She removed her shawl to reveal a proud, handsome face, one that was instantly recognized by most of the Sunday faithful.

The preacher was startled but also delighted by her sudden appearance. "My heavens," he announced in a deep, billowing voice. "If it isn't Moses herself, Miss Harriet Tubman, come to pay us a visit." Some members of the congregation gasped with excitement over this celebrity in their midst.

"Miss Harriet," the preacher beckoned, "what brings you to our beautiful corner of the world?"

Harriet spun around, searching the faces of the people in church, until she found the one she was looking for. In the third pew on the left hand side, there was a young woman in her early thirties, a beautiful woman named Irene. Harriet walked over to her and they embraced.

Then she turned to the preacher and said, "I come here today to bring the good news. I've traveled very far through dangerous lands, and I'm happy to have made it here to your wonderful community."

"Amen," some churchgoers called out.

"And I come today bringing a gift," she continued. "The greatest gift of all."

The door opened behind her and a boy entered. He walked in slowly, but once he saw his mother, he started to run.

"My boy! My boy!" Irene began sobbing at the sight of her long-lost son. She ran and met Pierre halfway down the aisle, and Pierre jumped into his mother's arms and gave her the biggest hug in all the world. ♣

"He's coming, he's coming!" Jack yelled as he ran down the hill. He had spotted the carriage through his spyglass, and by his estimation it would arrive in about ten minutes.

"All right, you all know what to do. Places everyone!" Marco called out to the assembled townspeople.

The carriage pulled into Neffs around three in the afternoon, the day after Gale had left the White House. The trip itself had been comfortable, and Gale had enjoyed seeing the farmland and rolling hills. He looked out the window and saw the big church in the distance. He figured Jack's family would not know he was coming, but he hoped they would be willing to take him in as Jack had said they would.

The carriage came to a stop a quarter of a mile outside of the town's central plaza. The driver came around and opened the door. "I was instructed to stop here," the driver said to Gale. "It was a pleasure giving you a ride, and I hope you enjoyed your trip."

"Yes, thank you," Gale said as he got out. The carriage pulled away and Gale was left by himself on the empty street. Sleepy little town, he thought. There was no one in sight in any direction. He walked toward the church, and soon the town came into view. Still, he saw no one.

Suddenly he heard a trumpet directly overhead. It was so loud and startling that he literally flinched. He turned toward the church and took a few steps back. There was a man in the bell tower playing a long trumpet, and he was dressed like a member of a European court. The man stopped playing momentarily and called out, "Ladies and Gentlemen, the Jack of Diamonds!"

Gale turned toward the city street, and he was stunned by what he saw. People had lined up on both sides, and they were smiling and applauding as he walked by. It was a hero's welcome for the champion Hearts player who had also managed to save the life of the President of the United States.

Toward the end of the welcome line, he spotted Jack, Celine, and Marco. Jack ran over to him and gave him a big bear hug. Celine and Marco followed, and though he had never been much of a hugger, he was very happy to see his friends again. He was also shocked and thrilled to see Raindrop, his loyal horse, standing beside them.

"I don't how you did it," Jack said, "but I want to hear all about it! Perhaps over dinner tonight. I hope you like spaghetti and meatballs!"

Jack introduced Gale to his mother and father, and they also embraced him in warm Italian fashion.

"Faremo mangiare bene stasera!" Jack's mother said excitedly.

"In other words, bring your appetite," Jack translated.

"Don't worry about me. I'm starving," Gale said.

And with that, the town of Neffs officially welcomed their newest citizen. ♣

She stood on the balcony and let the cool ocean breeze blow through her long dark hair. On the table next to her was her crown. As she picked it up and put it on her head, she closed her eyes, imagining for a moment the feeling of power and control she so desired. Someday, she told herself, it would all be hers. She would return from exile and assume her rightful place as the leading monarch of her era. She had been so close, and that was what made her failure all the more frustrating. But she would be patient. After all, her family had been waiting for centuries to achieve global hegemony, so a few years would be but a minor blip.

As she opened her eyes and looked at the calm sea, she thought of him. She never trusted him, and she knew he had not trusted her, but there was something about him that was irresistible. Somewhere in the recesses of whatever heart she had left was a small part of her that felt like they could have had a chance together.

But that was a dream. She was not built for relationships, and neither was he, for he could not resist the attention of other women, and she could not truly care about someone other than herself. And then there were the rumors of what he did to her son.

He would not find the treasure without the Jack of Spades, of that she was fairly certain. She did not know where the Jack was— *probably with one of those brats.* But no matter, she thought. Someday she would get her card back, and all the others too.

It was a cloudy day in the coastal Welsh town of Swansea, and the air from the bay was warm. The Coronado Kid arrived full of confidence after having made the long journey from the Mississippi River to Wales. He had always known from his own Jack of Hearts that the treasure was in Swansea, but now he knew it lay at the intersection of High Street and Low Street. Despite his relationship with Brunhilde, he had been unable to secure her complete trust, so he never got a look at the Jack of Spades. But how important could it be? The intersection he sought could not be that big.

After landing in Swansea, he got something to eat from the first tavern he found and then set out to find High Street and Low Street. It was a big town, and so he stopped by a cartographer's store and bought a map. He left the store and found a nearby bench to sit on where he eagerly opened the map.

He was shocked and dismayed at what he saw. There was High Street, and there was Low Street, but they did not just intersect: they weaved back and forth, crossing each other in figure eight patterns and intersecting seven different times. He cursed under his breath. What would he do now? He couldn't just dig up seven different city blocks! But he had come all the way here, so he had to try something.

He walked in the direction of the twisted streets and eventually got to one of the intersections. He was planning his next move when, from afar, he heard a voice he recognized.

"Spread out, in teams of three. I know he's here. I know it."

The Kid had good instincts and had always trusted them, and he immediately climbed the nearest tree: an odd-looking, crooked thing with a big U-shaped bend in the middle of the trunk. He scampered up to the top and looked down through the thick foliage. It was Hickok, his old rival, who had come all the way to Swansea to hunt him down and settle an old score.

Well, this certainly put a damper on his treasure-hunting plans, but it did not mean that he would have to be caught. He looked down at the many men who were scouring like ants in search of a crumb. He patted the bark with his hand and gave thanks for finding such an old, sturdy tree at exactly the right time. ♣

eline wins again!"

The young Wisconsinite happily referred to herself in the third person as she defeated Jack, Gale, and Marco at a second consecutive game of Hearts. The sun was starting to go down, and the outdoor air was warm and inviting.

"Best three out of five?" Jack pleaded.

"She's good," Marco noted. "You beat her on the boat?"

"Why couldn't I have played like this back then?" she bemoaned. "Then I'd be the one who was rich and famous!"

"I just wanted to make sure you won a few, so you didn't feel too bad about yourself," Jack said with a smile. Celine showed her appreciation for his teasing by giving him a tiny punch on the arm.

"Let's at least play one more before the sun goes down," Jack requested. They were able to get in a few more hands before it was too dark to see, so they called the last game with Jack as the winner.

"This night is so clear," Celine said. "Let's go check out the stars!"

They made their way to the top of a hill that looked down over the church and the town square. They lay down on their backs in the grass, and Celine snuggled next to Jack while Gale and Marco put their hands behind their heads and turned their gaze to the heavens. It was as clear a night as it could be, and the stars filled the entire sky in a symphony of light.

"Can you imagine if the president had been murdered?" Jack wondered. "What would have happened to our country?"

"You told me about the Lost Kingdom that Pierre described," Marco said. "I venture to say that had Lincoln died, someday many generations from now people would similarly call his a Lost Kingdom."

They sat quietly for a few minutes just observing the beautiful night sky. "Do you think Kingman will ever find that treasure?" Celine asked, breaking the silence.

Gale pulled the Jack of Spades from his pocket and looked it over. "I don't think so," he said. "Not without this."

"I have a feeling we haven't seen the last of our friends from the Hearts and Spades families," Jack speculated.

"So if the legend is to be believed," Marco said, "that night on the steamboat, the championship game was a battle between the legacies of the four old kingdoms of Europe... and between the four suits in the deck of cards."

"And once again, the good suits came out on top!" Jack said happily.

"Your families have a right to that treasure," Celine said. "I just know you'll find it someday."

"So what did Pierre tell you happened after they left Germania?" Marco asked.

"He didn't tell us much, only that they had a great nighttime parade," Celine responded. "And that the rest of it was a whole other story altogether."

"A nighttime parade? What must that have been like?" Marco wondered.

"It must have been something to see, that's for sure," Jack said.

♙

"Look Ma, it's starting!" a young girl called out.

People filled up both banks of the Thames in anticipation of the great celebration: a nighttime parade of boats that would be the first of its kind.

The royals returned to London with a mild sense of shock over the events of the previous week. It seemed an odd time to have a celebration, but it was King Harold's wisdom that proved valuable here.

The king reckoned that the people were looking for leadership now more than ever, and he wanted to reassure them that they were in good hands and that the kingdom was still intact. Even if it had been weakened by the defection of the Spades, it was still strong and a force to be reckoned with.

So the king called for a grand parade as a way to boost morale and show that the royal family was not going anywhere. Numerous boat floats were constructed with beautiful designs and floral arrangements, and there were fires burning on each one so that they would be visible at night. There was also music from strings and harpsichords filling the air.

"Look Ma, there's the King and Queen," the young girl said.

The last floats of the parade were the ones with the royal families.

First, there was King Harold and Queen Violet, and the king smiled and waved to the people while holding his trademark axe. Next came King Francesco, Queen Giovanna, and Prince Giuseppe, who was enjoying every minute of it. The young boy had been resilient in the face of danger, and it was his actions that had played a major role in the survival of the kingdom.

The next float's occupant was not as enthused. Was it his injury, the death of his parents, or something else that was dampening Prince Enrique's mood? Whatever the cause, he seemed to be going through the motions and counting the hours when he would return to España as the new king.

And finally, the last float belonged to the future king, Curtis Wellington and his soon-to-be bride, Princess Daphne. Curtis had been smitten with Daphne from the beginning, and they had grown even closer on the ride home. He knew that she was the one he wanted to marry, and he did not waste any time in asking her the big question.

"This is wonderful!" he said to her while smiling and waving to the people of London. He took a moment to look up at the sky. It was a clear night, and the stars twinkled brightly. There were four stars clustered together, a little brighter than the others. He imagined they represented the four families, and he thought it sad that the kingdom had lost a star. He also thought of Edward, who had arrived with them in London but then immediately said his goodbyes, disappearing back into the shadows.

Curtis's thoughts were interrupted by a shooting star that traveled right through the four-star constellation. "Did you see that?" he asked Daphne.

"Yes, it was spectacular," she said. "Maybe it's a sign that there's hope for the kingdom after all."

Gale closed his eyes and pictured himself at the parade so many years ago. He opened his eyes and looked back up at the sky. He had been through so much in the last week. He had won the greatest card tournament in the land. He had accumulated more money than he knew what to do with. And he had saved the president's life.

He turned his head to look at his new friends lying in the grass alongside him. Of all that had befallen him, what truly made him happiest was that he had found some great friends, a community, and a home.

He turned his attention back to the sky and saw the same moon he had seen earlier in the week over the painted desert. And then there was the figurative moon—the one that he had so gloriously shot at the Hearts table on the steamboat. The moon in the sky had been waning, but off to its left, there were four stars that shone a little more brightly than the others.

The number four was significant to his people. Four elements of the earth. Four directions on the land. Four seasons in a year. And four suits in a deck. Diamonds, Clubs, Hearts, and Spades.

Looked at a certain way, the four stars looked a little like the shape of a diamond, and he could not help but smile. A diamond in the sky. ♦

ACKNOWLEDGEMENTS

To the following people I give my sincerest thanks:

Caroline Sweedo, Walter Sweedo, Elizabeth Sweedo, Lara Dolphin, Maria Samaritano, Phil Gonzales, and Alex Schroeder. Thank you for offering to read my unfinished manuscript and for your feedback, and a special thanks to Alex for providing a valuable teenage perspective.

Kristin Mitchell and the team at Little Creek Press for your high-quality work and for everything you have done in publishing this book. Thanks to Carl Stratman for a fantastic editing job, and Michael Kress-Russick for an amazing cover design.

Sarah Young, for helping me to find the courage necessary to take a risk.

Katie Green, author of *Sierra Summer, 1874*, for inviting me into your home to talk about publishing. Grazie mille, Elena Bender, for your help with Italian translations.

D-Money, Schober, and The Dog, for hours of fun and inspiration around the Hearts table, even when you team up against me or when you thwart my lunar missions.

And most of all, thank you to my wife and my son. I could never have done this without your love and support. ♣

ABOUT THE AUTHOR

Nicholas Sweedo grew up in Pennsylvania and now lives in Wisconsin. In his spare time, he enjoys history, sports, and shooting the moon. Visit www.thenightingalemoon.com to learn more. ♣